UNCONQUERED SOULS

UNCONQUERED SOULS

THE RESISTENTIALISTS

C. L. SULZBERGER

THE OVERLOOK PRESS
Woodstock New York

Copyright © 1963, 1973 by C. L. Sulzberger

Chapter 1 appeared in shorter and
different form in *Saga* in 1963.

First published in 1973 by
The Overlook Press, Inc.
Lewis Hollow Road
Woodstock, New York 12498

*Published simultaneously in Canada by
The Macmillan Company of Canada, Limited*

SBN 0-87951-004-8

Library of Congress Catalog Card Number: 72-81087

Printed in the United States of America

R. I. P.

CONTENTS

INTRODUCTION

HOW THINGS ARE AGAINST US

My home town of Paris is notable for the ideologies it nourishes: its dadaism, its surrealism, its existentialism. It was here that the excellently eccentric poet Gérard de Nerval strode up and down the boulevards leading a lobster on a leash or, when he preferred, a suckling pig with the Pope's face limned on its pink behind. One after another, gay and bitter, serious and sardonic, hopeful and despairing, in this city where a donkey won an art prize with a work dribbled out of paint buckets by its tail, these movements have sprung up like mushrooms.

Not so many years ago, there flourished among more profound, more penetrating and more pretentious theories a jocular idea, a literary gag self-mockingly called Resistentialism. The slogan of the Resistentialists was simply this: "Les choses sont contre nous—things are against us."

A good Resistentialist knew he was playing life's game with a deck of cards carefully stacked against him. If he dropped a piece of toast, it always landed butter side down. If he bet on a horse, it was scratched before the race began. If there was one fly in a café, it fell into his beer. If he waited in a movie queue, all the seats were filled just as he reached the ticket booth.

And yet the Resistentialist survived. If things were against him, he too was against things. He had durability. He could see how he was condemned to be tricked by what he perceived as fate; but he managed, nonetheless, to persevere, whether with humor, with grimness or with plain obstinacy. If he could not conquer things, things at least could never completely conquer him, even when things showered down like Biblical plagues or crushed him like a juggernaut.

The quintessence of the Resistentialist is this survival capacity. His soul despairs. His brain becomes dull marrow wired by sensitive, throbbing nerves. He has no hope, no faith, no crutch with which to hobble down destiny's path. And still he endures, the Resistentialist; thanks to the quality of his courage, he resists.

It was Hemingway who contributed that recent cliché on courage: grace under pressure. But this is inadequate. Generally the Resistentialist has little grace. What he has, perhaps, is will, the will not to triumph but merely to exist, to make the best of bad things, of all those incalculable and dreadful things that hover on fate's threshold, ready to descend.

Life, from the very start, makes its mark upon the true Resistentialist, and he but rarely makes a proper mark on life. He is too busy simply surviving and too predestined to disaster to avoid it, a doomed, unlucky fellow, butter side down.

I have written here of three such men, three persistent, valiant, undaunted men, each of whom withstood with gallantry the gaunt years of misfortune, impossible adversity and cruel strain. They weren't really graceful but, Lord, they were unyielding, in one way or another. And, in the end, each could at least boast like the Abbé Sieyès, when asked what he did during the French Revolution's Terror, "I lived."

I have written of these three men in what might be called the novella form—except that everything I say herein happens to be true. These are real stories about real men who endured incredibly real events. And each took part in one of the major movements of our stirring era, played a vigorous role in that movement and ultimately was destroyed by it.

We have a Communist who fought some of Communism's bloodiest battles and rose to great eminence in Communism's ranks—and then was destroyed by Communism. We have a warrior-artist who might well by heritage have been a Fascist and yet who devoted all his life to fighting Fascism—only to be squashed by Fascism when both he and it were dead. And we have a soldier, an audacious fighting man who scorned and courted death in war, merely to elude it and to be undone by war when it, in fact, was over.

These men came from different nations, were born into different circumstances and pursued entirely different courses for different reasons. Yet they were bound together by their Resistentialism, by their courage and ability to survive. Each was brilliantly brave in moments of great stress and unexcelled upon the battlefield; but none was truly remarkable in peace.

The artist, a man of considerable talent and rare discrimination, was nevertheless no great artist. He resented being condemned to live in the shadow, for example, of painters like Jackson Pollock. But he never managed to impress his thoughts upon our times with a talent sufficient to his aspirations and intentions.

The Communist was perceptive enough to discover the flaws in a system he helped establish and, for a period, helped rule. But in the last analysis he became for history nothing save a modest historian.

And the soldier, a peaceable little fellow who never even won a decoration although he deserved the highest, earned by his efforts contumely and disgrace. Still, all of them, each in his own way, resisted right to the bitter borders of despair. None of them succumbed. They kept a private integrity intact in a savage world.

Their paths were diverse: the artist, brought up in a most devout creed, was failed by that creed when he most needed it, although he was already dead. The soldier, a pathetic, small and simple man, had no belief save in a slightly tawdry love—and was deserted by its object. And the Communist, shorn of his ideology and detesting it, continued formally to adhere to his godless god while talking of nothing but the Christian ethic.

The period of which I write, so recent to most of those who will read of these strange happenings, is gone. Nations reflected in these pages as enemies are now seen in another looking glass. The Germans are our allies; the Spanish are our friends; and even the Communist Yugoslavs are regarded as benevolent folk in the altered pattern of politics. But let us not forget what passing time does to those it encompasses in its passage.

*   *   *

This book itself has had a kind of Resistentialist history. When I first committed it to paper more than a decade ago, I was innocent enough not to know that letters belonged to the men who wrote them, not to the recipient, and my then publisher foolishly did not advise me of this legal tradition. Therefore, although Ernest Hemingway had, in fact, more than once suggested that I publish the story of "The Bravest Collaborator" and although he was still alive at that time, I did not ask for his permission to print his letters to me on the subject. It was only after his sad death that I learned he had left a special instruction that none of his correspondence should be published.

By then the book had already been written, edited, almost formally published. However, it promptly ran into trouble from an unexpected quarter. Vlado Dedijer was deeply upset about its appearance (I had mailed him a copy) and claimed that it would jeopardize his position inside Yugoslavia. He had recently been granted permission to go abroad with his family, after the appalling tragedy of his little boy's suicide, and he feared my book might make it impossible for him to return if, later on, he should wish to do so.

When I first heard of this in Paris I immediately telephoned my publisher in New York and asked him to suspend publication. I later met with Dedijer at the American Embassy in London, brought together by my close and highly esteemed friend David Bruce, then U.S. Ambassador, and it was blatantly evident that Vlado was in a highly nervous and overwrought condition. At the same time I learned from General "Buck" Lanham that Mary Hemingway, the author's widow, contemplated making difficulties if Ernest's letters were textually reprinted. So I gave up and asked that in spite of all the prepublication expenses incurred, the publishers forgo issuance of the work; this, in spite of its importance to me as a historical comment. But, as the years went by, the book remained on my mind.

Now, many years later, endless water has flowed under the bridge of time and I have wished to resurrect this testament to courage: the courage of Michel Dupont (which is a pseudonym, selected to avoid embarrassment, as the reader will soon understand); the courage of Vlado and Olga and Vera Dedijer and of Milovan Djilas who all remained true to their ideals and individual faiths despite the pressures of a hard war and harder revolution; and the courage of Rudoph von Ripper which, like so many brave tales of our times, is known by only a handful and which his wife and friends wished to have at least in some small degree memorialized.

The moment has come, I feel, to correct an injustice, to remind a later generation that indeed there once was a World War II during which a hideous form of dictatorship, unimaginably brutal, was foisted upon the earth's most civilized continent and this dreadful, leaden confinement lasted for approximately five years, five years during which millions of people were slaughtered, tortured, starved, imprisoned or simply deprived of their humanity. That magnificent cluster of civilizations known as "Europe" was almost wholly obliterated or crippled, intellectually, physically and above all morally. Thousands of men and women silently accepted as inescapable a degrading tyranny and, indeed, many even ceased to pray secretly for its end. Whole countries such as much of France, the beacon of liberty and liberality, became paralyzed as the French themselves are only now beginning to confess to each other, witness the 1971 movie *The Sorrow and the Pity*, a film which deeply disturbed them by its revelations of collaboration.

The famous heroes of this terrifying time of trouble have their names inscribed on history's Golden Roll: de Gaulle, Churchill, Zhukov, Tito and the more renowned underground leaders in each occupied land whose legends, together with those of their chieftains both in Europe and rescuing America, are nationally as well as internationally known. But the little man who loses most and gains least in vast conflicts and who is, if ever remembered, soonest forgotten, has already become an un-person despite his suffering. This book is for the most part about that ordinary human being. And it was first conceived many years ago when the continent was still filled with lean men and women home from the war and the leaner ones back from the concentration camps.

But why tell these tales all these years later? What importance? After all, how many other thousands of Resistentialists have there been since, above all in Asia, Africa or Latin America? Were not the few who followed Che into the Bolivian jungle Resistentialists of a sort? And those who stormed into Havana with Fidel, many among them later to feel deceived? Are those Greeks arrested by the Nazis and exiled by the Colonels qualified for this description? Or the latest generation of Czechoslovakia's Good Soldier Schweiks? Or the Vietnamese who in turn and at times simultaneously fought Japan, France, the United States and each other? War is a way of life in their incredibly hard land. And how many untold millions of Resistentialists have existed for all those generations spread out earlier until the dawn of mankind? A man with sap in his veins is almost doomed thereby to be one of that ilk; for fortune smiles consistently on but a rare few.

I have thought it worth making permanent these histories of how ordinary men can and do resist great tribulations or, if they bend with them, still rise again. Every generation, as we learn far too young, has its ample quantities of Jobs and the generation of which I write, which fought and then digested World War II, had them by the thousand. It is simply my fortune that I knew a handful of these men, that by rare accident I learned of their deeds of heroism, most of which would remain anonymous in the unknown annals of a rapidly forgotten era, were I not now to speak about and for them.

None of these are great giants in the earth, and indeed all the Resistentialists herein described are simple people to a greater or lesser degree, with the blazing exception of Djilas. His finely honed talent and unconquerable soul lift him to a special eminence that must for many decades hence escape the impressive amnesia of time.

But these tales, I believe, contain poignant examples of unconquerability. Each Resistentialist showed to one or another degree that although he was in no sense master of his fate, he still remained captain of his soul. I am therefore pleased that at last this book of mine now sees the light of day since it brings back some memory of the terror that clanked down upon this world a generation ago and of the excruciating cost paid by those determined to survive.

CHAPTER 1

THE RIPPER

"The last of the great romantics are dying. Ripper has gone; soon it will be you and me."

—ANDRÉ MALRAUX

The most striking couple I have ever known:

HE: About five feet ten inches tall, heavy set, with buck teeth and one nearly blind wall eye, which produces a rather wild expression; strong hands, with half the right index finger missing; a mustache of the Edwardian cavalry variety, twirlable ends cut off; a distinct Teutonic accent; great charm of manner; immense cultivation and knowledge of the subtleties of food and wine; a fascination with and for women; a dandy in dress; a fondness for sports cars and fast driving; a great soul, much energy, and a weak, overstrained heart; the dreams and aspirations of an artist; unexcelled personal courage and the instincts and abilities of a killer.

SHE: Six feet tall in her bare feet, myopic; blonde and beautiful almost beyond comparison; stands very straight and wears the highest possible heels; always immaculately coiffed and, when swimming, meanders placidly along, carefully made-up face and golden curls erect out of the water, like some lovely sea creature of mythology; a slender, lithesome body and long, long legs; full red mouth, aristocratic hands and features; encyclopedic knowledge of books, paintings and music and an almost professional talent on the flute; charm, humor, dry wit and a fantastic capacity for alcohol; a taste for clothes and jangling jewelry that only she could wear; attractive to all living men and, like her husband, a fiercely true friend.

These are the surface impressions of Baron Rudolph Karl von Ripper and his wife Evelyn, or Avi, and this tale concerns them.

I first met Rip, or The Ripper, as he was variously called, early in 1944 when an American army, beside polyglot allies, English, French, Canadian and Polish, was trying to fight its way northward in Italy—northward from Naples to the Gustav Line, which Hitler's forces, seeking to stem the tide, had erected around the ancient monastery of Monte Cassino. Ripper's name at that time was almost legendary.

The G.I.'s used to tell of a strange German in American uniform who would disappear for days behind the Nazi lines, killing silently with a knife the enemies he found, then stealing back to the nearest U.S. division, where he would deliberately stumble on a startled sentry.

"Who goes there?"

And then the guttural, accented answer: "Rudolph von Ripper."

The sentry would inevitably escort "another goddamned Kraut" to squad command, to platoon and thence a lieutenant would telephone battalion headquarters: "We've got some strange gink here who wears our uniform but speaks like a Fritz." And a bored voice would reply: "His name isn't by any chance von Ripper?"

"My God, how did you know?"

"Well, just turn the bastard loose and tell him to stop being a nuisance."

During that winter and early, intolerably cold spring, I would occasionally sit in poker games with Ernie Pyle, that excellent correspondent, other colleagues and this incredible individual, Rip, who seemed mild and merry, more concerned with young girls, a well-cooked meal, a bottle of brandy and long conversations on modern painting than with the genius for killing so widely associated with his name.

I lost track of Ripper late that bloody spring when I flew to Russia. Next I heard that he had taken a parachutist course for the O.S.S. near Bari together with my youthful cousin Peter Payne. Rip was then in his late thirties, slightly overweight, and a good deal overage compared to the youngsters jumping with him. Peter went on to drop into Albania as a British captain, where he helped the local Partisans liberate the town of Elbasan.

He told me of this eccentric fellow, Rip, who when they were instructed by the jump sergeant in their very first session that it was necessary at all costs to relax, promptly found himself a South Italian girl, shacked up with her in one of those beehive huts discovered only in Apulia, and would appear daily, filled with booze, satiated with pleasure, entirely loose to jump. Peter said it was oddly disconcerting to see Ripper's pop eyes staring madly in two different directions simultaneously as he slid sadly out the door when the jump master called his name.

I again saw Rip, by then a captain, in Paris a few weeks after the European war had ended. It was at the immense *hotel particulier* of Comtesse de Y., one of his former girl friends, a mansion filled with an extraordinary collection of paintings, a strange hodgepodge, Goya hanging beside Picasso, Rubens next to Dali, and Bérard precisely on top of Burne-Jones.

Ripper was filled with joy. His first wife, Mops, had just come to Paris from Sweden after having been interned in the dreadful Nazi concentration camp of Ravensbrück. He was, of course, glad to see her. But he was even more glad because now, at last, they could arrange the divorce each of them desired. So he was drinking vast quantities of champagne and, in his delight, performing the unusual trick of devouring each glass as soon as he had emptied it. His buck teeth ground and ground away and he swallowed the pulverized glass with seeming relish, explaining as he nibbled Venetian goblets that "green tastes better than any other color."

Over the years we became close friends. He married the magnificent Avi and lived with her right after the war in an artsy-crafty Connecticut barn. She worked as an art critic and he resumed his chosen profession of painter. Until then I had seen little of his work save for a sardonic and expensive book of political etchings, called *Ecrasez l'Infame*, satirizing Hitler, which he had done before the war.

Comtesse de Y. had managed to hide a copy during the occupation.

In 1947 the Rippers came to stay with us for a fortnight in Paris. He was then arranging for the first modern art exhibit, since the 1938 Anschluss, to be shown in Vienna, where he had spent much of his youth and which he had later helped to liberate. Somehow or other he managed to persuade American and European collectors to entrust him with valuable paintings and sculptures and these began rapidly to clutter up our flat: works by Jackson Pollock, Kandinsky, Brancusi, Giacometti; a long list of artists whose renown had mushroomed while the Viennese stultified under Hitler's heel and to whom Rip wished to introduce the citizens of his birthland.

The day before he and Avi drove off in two cars with their garish and valuable display we gave them a large cocktail party. Rip destroyed a magnum of champagne and gobbled up the glasses. Then he pulled his right arm from his coat sleeve, inserted a gnarled, wrought-iron Giacometti arm in its place, a sculpture that looked like the limb of a scoriaceous Pompeii skeleton, and greeted all arriving guests by shaking their hands with this. Next morning they drove off, sadly hung over, their autos packed to the roof with fantastic art treasures. They crossed the French-Swiss and Swiss-Austrian borders without trouble, Lord knows how. Afterward I learned that none of the exhibit was insured. It was worth a great deal of money.

Later Rip, who had become an American citizen thanks to his wartime exploits, settled for some time in Vienna as

an art professor at the university. Still later he and Avi
bought a splendid house at Pollensa, on the Spanish island
of Majorca. They furnished it with taste and originality and
settled down, he to his painting and she to her books and
flute. In addition to painting, to earn his living he
began to design flamboyant jewelry, the kind his wife
adored, and to draw cartoons for original rugs, which he
had woven by a tapestry firm in Barcelona. He himself
would purchase precious and semi-precious stones to em-
bellish the complex seashell and leaf designs of his jewelry.

About twice each year Ripper and Avi would descend on
us in Paris to sell his creations, enjoy the good life or take
off on further journeys, sometimes to his old baroness
mother in Salzburg, sometimes around the world, sometimes just to North or South America. Once he took several
months off to travel as a kind of bodyguard and pimp to an
assemblage of Salvador Dali jewelry, which included a
mechanical, beating ruby heart and which was displayed to
the chic and tasteless elements of society. Rip courted these
latter as a businessman and held them in contempt as an
artist.

Lee Ault, an American connoisseur, wrote in the cata-
logue of von Ripper's 1961 New York painting exhibition:
"Ripper served, at various times during his stormy life, as
propagandist, soldier, lecturer and bon vivant extraordinary.
His thirst for experience was insatiable and led him inevitably to such unlikely pursuits as the French Foreign Legion, circus harlequin, inmate of Oranienburg and keeper
of the Dali jewels.

"Nevertheless, despite such digressions from the field

of pure art, his capacity for expression was constantly being renewed and he was able to produce etchings, jewelry design, tapestries and painting of the highest order. Such a variegation of talent led some to think of him as an anachronism, a kind of twentieth century 'Renaissance Man,' and others to write him off less kindly as a gifted dilettante or soldier of fortune. Neither appraisal could have been farther from the truth.

"From his early satirical etchings (inspired by Nazi crime and political oppression) to these paintings of the latter years, Ripper's consuming interest was art and his ambition to become a fulltime creative painter. He . . . preferred to develop his theme gradually until an orchestration of mankind with the world around him had been achieved—semiabstracted in a highly individualized style, yet warmly human in its effect.

"These pictures of the last decade speak glowingly for themselves. No interpreter is needed. They are the voice of a remarkable man and a strongly creative artist, one who will be missed by those who knew him and came to understand his work."

For Ripper is now dead; and this is the story of his life and death, the bravest man I have known and as loyal as any; a killer who resented being reminded of the fact but whose name, for those of us in the English-speaking world, was by some weird accident so aptly chosen; an artist who perhaps never fulfilled himself, maybe for lack of time, more probably because he was born into the wrong era. He should have come to maturity in Hapsburg days, before the Balkan wars, and burned out his life with splendid insouciance during the golden age of Scott Fitzgerald.

In a letter to this writer, the brilliant French author André Malraux said of Rip:

"He was a man of talent, courage and kindness. If these three qualities are rather widespread, they rarely come together. As for the courage he displayed in several countries while serving a single cause with distracted relentlessness, you have undoubtedly said the essential.

"Nevertheless, I should like to add a color to your design: for this democratic patrician, from whom emanated a contagious likableness and a willingness to help, courage was inseparable from good humor. If this is not the greatest praise one can give to an artist fighter, it is at least one of the rarest; and perhaps the most moving."

Baron Rudolf Karl Hugo von Ripper (later Americanized to Rudolph Charles) was born in 1904 at Klausenburg (now Cluj) in what is today Rumanian Transylvania but was then a provincial capital in the Austro-Hungarian empire. His father, Baron Eduard Maria von Ripper, was the last aide-de-camp to the Hapsburg Emperor. His mother, Countess Claire von Salis-Samaden, came from a much higher rank in the snobbish Central European aristocracy and her family frowned upon the marriage. But Eduard was known as the handsomest general in the Austrian Army and this was enough for him to press his suit successfully.

Ripper's ancestors, who came from the country nobility, had almost all by tradition chosen a military career. His grandfather was marshal of the imperial court. He supervised the education of the last Grand Duke of Tuscany, a Hapsburg, before dying in the battle of Koeniggraetz. Ripper himself, although he fought in three armies, never served the Hapsburg Empire, which collapsed around him when he was fourteen, the year his father died of cancer.

He was a troubled boy, born with the handicap of one wall eye, which, while not entirely blind, was incapable of focusing. His childhood showed a tremendous conflict between inherited influences and artistic instincts. From the age of three he began to sketch. Once, when he was ill with influenza, his mother found him standing naked before a mirror drawing a self-portrait. He became a good horseman and enjoyed riding two Trakehner steeds. He also was entranced by the gardens on the family estate and used to tell his mother: "I want to find out why this is so beautiful and magical." When he was bothered or when rice pudding was placed before him (a dish he loathed) he would automatically run a fever. This infuriated the sense of discipline of his father, who placed Ripper, at the age of ten, as a page at the Emperor's court.

After the old general was carried to his grave, covered with decorations, and postwar chaos set in, the local commander at Salzburg (where Ripper was then living with his mother and sister) called for volunteers to guard government buildings. Ripper, although only fourteen, volunteered for service and joined a mounted patrol. This first military experience, his only one in Austrian uniform, lasted ten days. But, combined with the absence of his father's stern hand, it gave him a new sense of independence.

The immediate consequence was his expulsion from the Jesuit school he attended and, soon afterward, from two other institutions. At that point he informed his mother:

"I am now the head of the family and the boss." His mother refused to acknowledge this authority so he ran away from home, first to Innsbruck and then to Berlin, where he lived in a furnished room in a workers' district. He first got a job in a sawmill. He abandoned this when a traveling circus appeared and offered him work, originally as a barker, then as cashier, then as a clown, his role being to pull an artificial rat out of his baggy pants. He also fell in love, for the first time, with a dark-haired equestrienne.

After some weeks with the circus he quit and traveled to Duisburg, an industrial town in the Rhineland. There he found employment as a carpenter's helper in a coal mine. He saved enough money to buy paints and brushes and studied at the near-by Duesseldorf Academy. Later he moved to Bonn and painted, finally returning to his mother's home at the age of nineteen. He became restless and moved to Paris in 1923, living in Montparnasse and spending most of his time at the old Café de Dôme.

The life in Paris of the twenties was gay and stimulating but Ripper spent more money than he earned. So he went to Lyon, was entranced by a Foreign Legion recruiting poster and decided to volunteer. He signed up in 1925 for a five-year stretch and was sent steerage to Tunis. There he was assigned to a cavalry regiment at Sidi-el-Hani, near Kairouan. He didn't like the life, much as he adored the desert with its glowing colors. He wrote his mother: "I live in an oasis, blue and gray and gold." He never forgot the contorted faces of his fellow soldiers dying from the bites of tiny asps hiding among the rocks.

The Ripper

Rip first went to war when he was sent as a replacement to the Legion contingent fighting against Druse tribesmen in Syria and Lebanon. Very soon after his arrival, he was in an ambushed squadron and was wounded by bullets in the knee and left lung. He was evacuated back to Sidi-el-Hani. There he amused himself by drawing on stolen scraps of paper. He wrote to his mother: "Although I am never alone, I am always lonely. But loneliness is very necessary and makes it possible to stand the strangeness. All this must have its point. I realize I have signed up for five years but I have thought this over for a long time and I also realize I cannot imagine life without painting. And this is too long a time not to paint. My great problem here is not the life, which is hard but fine. It is that I cannot work and I must." He concluded: "Life is not often easy, even when one is young. Fate is often stronger than the greatest will. I always have plans and fantasies. This is the only thing that counts, to dream; because, in life, one can never realize those marvelous dreams. There is no money here; a little money is freedom; talent is liberty; and liberty is the greatest money there is."

Ripper determined on liberty at all costs. Difficult as it was to desert, he took French leave from the French Foreign Legion in 1926. After receiving some money from his mother, he obtained a one-day travel permit, forged a new date to it, went to Sousse and then Tunis, purchased white linen pants, a gray pullover and blue beret, one by one, in the Arab bazaar, changed behind a clump of bushes in a park, left his uniform there and boarded a train for Algiers.

There he filled a suitcase and canvas bag with straw, got in line with some stevedores whose papers were not scrutinized, and clambered onto a Dutch ship.

He spent the summer in Austria and Berlin. After a brief affair with an actress, he pooled resources with a friend, bought some movie equipment, and started off for Djibouti, Indo-China and Bali to make documentary films. In Bali he ran into an American acquaintance who had him invited aboard a yacht bound for China.

How strange a country was the China of those days, carved into so many spheres of influence among the intricate alliances of foreign powers, feudal barons and rapacious businessmen. That was the time when Stalin had his agents Borodin and Chuikov, the latter to become a famous marshal, scheming to take over and when the young Chiang Kai-shek staged his brutal Canton coup d'état against his Communist allies. It was a seething, teeming, evil China, replete with opium, spies, White Russian dancing girls, European profiteers, American missionaries, the clatter of man-drawn rickshaws, the rattle of spars on creaking junks, the snick-snack of mah-jong counters, the sweep of silk-clad courtesans, the yammer-yammer-yammer of the peddlers, the smell of garlic, of French perfume, and death.

That Christmas he was introduced to a man named Ellison, a Minnesota Scotsman who had once been a newspaperman but who had settled in Shanghai as a gun runner. He was engaged in the profitable trade of supplying arms to rival Chinese warlords. Ellison discovered that Ripper was a cousin of the director of Skoda, the Czechoslovakian munitions firm. He was then seeking a supply of light Skoda automatic weapons and hired Ripper as private secretary to help arrange the order. So Rip moved into Ellison's penthouse apartment in the old French concession of Shanghai and became, in fact, an arms agent, bodyguard and private procurer to his hard-boiled and successful boss.

Ellison, a burly, red-haired Middle Westerner, spoke ten Chinese dialects and always traveled with his private harem. He had a regular poker game twice a week with the famous Soong brothers, whose sisters married Sun Yat-sen and Chiang Kai-shek, and Rip was often assigned to sit in and play for his employer. Ellison also wore a bullet-proof vest because of the continual threat of assassination by rival arms merchants or disgruntled warlords.

This was interesting work for a footloose young man. Shipments were arranged through the French chief of police. This official bribed other international authorities so that barges could be loaded with guns and ammunition, shipped upstream under police escort and finally distributed to the junks or oxcarts of Chinese purchasers.

Ripper enjoyed this life of intrigue, adventure, buccaneering and corruption until the autumn of 1929. One evening he had a rendezvous with his boss at the Kit Kat Club, a dance dive where the poker games were held and where, that night, despite armored vest and armed bodyguards, Ellison was shot dead. Rip received a warning that he was next on the list, whereupon he cashed his bank account, gave a bungalow on the race course as a farewell present to his Chinese girl friend, and took off by Trans-Siberian railway across Russia to Austria.

This marked an end to the first phase of Ripper's career,

a phase of immature art and purposeless hazard, zestful but without true meaning. He was not to return to the Orient until shortly before he died, on a last gay global tour. And, in between, he learned the meaning of political terror and enlisted in a life-long fight against it that never ended, even with his death.

He spent the winter of 1929–1930 on the French Riviera. There he met an attractive German brunette named Dorothea Sternheim, the wealthy daughter of Karl Sternheim, a playwright and at that time a sort of Continental equivalent of Noël Coward. He married her in 1930 and they settled in Berlin.

The Berlin of those days, the Berlin of Christopher Isherwood, was a vigorous, bubbling but depraved city, living in a strange, frenzied fever, in dreadful shadows. Hitler was to take power just three years afterward. Every form of pleasurable vice was rampant. Both Ripper and Dorothea, who went by the nickname of Mops (the usual word for poodle), took to smoking opium. Ripper discovered that the drug was an erotic in light doses. He gradually became an addict and remained one for many months.

The young Austrian baron and his witty, attractive wife played an active part in Berlin society. But, on occasional trips to Paris, they became acquainted with a group of intellectuals, including several Communists, who were already working in an underground movement against the increasing Nazi threat. Ripper agreed to draw cartoons for them. He spent many weeks on Majorca in the Balearic Islands, working on these drawings.

After Hitler seized control of Germany in early 1933 he

returned to Paris. There he agreed to help his anti-Nazi friends prepare a famous political pamphlet called the Brown Book which described Nazi brutalities. He smuggled a thousand copies of this brochure, under covers stamped with the title of Goethe's *Hermann and Dorothea*, into Germany in his own baggage when he returned to Berlin, this time without Mops, who had found another friend.

On October 3, 1933, a decisive day, Ripper was living in a comfortable pension on the Kurfuerstendamm. He came home from a late formal dinner, took sedatives and was fast asleep when two men in dark overcoats and hats burst in, turned on the lights, pulled aside their jackets to disclose shoulder holsters, announced themselves as "Gestapo" and ordered him to dress and go with them. Sadly reflecting that he needed a haircut, Rip got dressed and went along. He was driven to the prison of the Secret State Police on Prinz Albrechtstrasse.

How few Americans can know just what this means: the late night knock upon the door, the drugged response, the shattered lock, the sudden blaze of lights, the strange, blank faces, the scream of tires as a car wheels off to an undetermined but surely hideous destination, the feeling of loneliness, of anonymity, of total isolation; the feeling that the impossible has happened.

The first interrogation was restrained and polite. To his surprise, after being fingerprinted and spending some hours in a solitary cell, Ripper was taken into a carpeted office where, behind a desk, sat a man of his acquaintance, dressed in the uniform of an S.S. colonel: Rudolf Diels, first chief of the Gestapo, then run by Goering. Both Ripper and Mops had known this man socially and Diels greeted him courteously in French as "mon cher Baron." He asked him to be seated and produced several copies of *Hermann and Dorothea*, the anti-Nazi Brown Book, found in Ripper's room among his shirts.

In flat tones he told him: "I am afraid, my dear Baron, that we must accuse you both of high treason and of preparations for high treason." Ripper replied it was impossible for an Austrian citizen to be charged with treason to Germany, a foreign land. He asked to be put in touch with his legation. Diels smiled. He nodded. And Ripper was taken off.

He was locked up in central Gestapo headquarters, the infamous Columbia House. Stripped of necktie, belt and shoe laces, he was hurled into a small cell furnished only with a sack of straw in one corner and a metal bowl. An S.S. guard in black uniform entered. He instructed his prisoner: "Stand at attention. And now remember this. Whenever the peephole on your door is lifted and light comes in, whatever the time, you will face the door and stand at attention. Dismissed." The lock slammed shut.

Next day he was beaten for the first time. Four guards came in and announced: "Prisoner 611, you are a swine who has committed high treason." One of them, surprisingly, then asked Ripper if he wished a cigarette. He was puzzled but said yes. The chief guard lit his own cigarette and then said: "611, we will now show you how we smoke here, or rather how you smoke here." The three other guards seized him, flung him down, and forced open his mouth. The chief carefully tore his cigarette in half and flung the lighted end into Ripper's mouth. Then he lit the remnant and repeated the performance. They did this several times and the burning was so great that tears poured down Ripper's cheeks. Finally one guard took up the metal bowl in the cell, urinated in it and said: "Poor fellow. It hurts him, doesn't it? We will put out the flames." And he poured the urine into Ripper's mouth. Then they beat him until he lay unconscious.

The following day, mouth burned and body bruised, he was interrogated. He denied he had been involved in any conspiracy and claimed the Brown Book could not have been found in his room or, if it had been, someone else had placed it there. He was called before Diels and this time he was told sternly to stand at attention. A strong light was focused on his face and Ripper could see himself mirrored in the glass covering a portrait of Hitler behind Diels' chair. When he again insisted he had had nothing to do with the propaganda material he saw Diels lift one eyebrow. At Ripper's back were standing two huge S.S. guards. He remembered seeing in the portrait-mirror one hand lifting upward. The next instant he felt a terrible blow. Two days later he regained consciousness in a hospital bed.

Ripper found himself in a room with three other men. There was no furniture save four beds, and the door and window were barred. The doctor, who was standing by him when he recovered his senses, said: "You were brought in by the Gestapo two nights ago. You are in a police hospital on the prisoners' floor. The S.S. men informed me you had had an accident, that a brick had fallen from a roof. I

33

know better than to believe this tale. I have a very good idea what hit you. But I don't want to know about it.

"I have no truck with the Gestapo. I am a doctor. I am here to help sick people and to try and cure them. It is unfortunate that this thing has happened to you. But I do not want to learn what you are involved in. I will help you as much as I can, as a doctor. I will give you the best available treatment and I will try to keep you here as long as possible. That is all I can do."

Ripper's skull had been fractured and bore a thick, ridged scar the rest of his life. Thanks to the doctor's insistence, he was allowed a fortnight to recover. Then he was returned to Columbia House and, almost immediately, summoned again by Diels.

Diels behaved as if nothing had happened. He sat impassively before the same portrait of the Fuehrer while the light blazed in Ripper's face. The Gestapo chief merely said: "You are foolish not to confess. You are foolish not to tell us who is involved with you in this plot. I am sorry, Baron, but there is nothing more I can do. Apparently your legation has no interest in you. You see, they have not even made an inquiry. I fear you will have to be judged."

Ripper was then marched between two black-shirt guards to the basement, where, in a small chamber, sat an S.S. officer wearing a judge's robe over his uniform. A judge's hat lay on his desk together with several file folders, a crucifix and two candles. Behind him, also, was a picture of Hitler.

He said: "You have been charged with high treason. If you think it makes any difference to us that you are Austrian, then you are wrong. You are part of the German people. We do not recognize Austria as a separate state." He reached for his hat, donned it and intoned: "Hereby I pronounce you convicted of high treason. The sentence for this crime is death."

Before Ripper could even appreciate what had happened, he was frog-marched down a corridor at the end of which was a wall covered with bloodstains and shredded with bullet holes. Facing the wall, he was tied to metal holders in it, and then behind him he heard heavy boots march up, heard the sound of rifle bolts being shot back, heard the guttural orders: "On the target. Aim. Fire!" He suddenly sensed rather than heard bullets crashing into the wall above his head. He vomited; there was laughter behind him; just a cruel Nazi joke. He was taken back to his cell and thrown inside.

A few days later he was brought into a hallway, where, to his astonishment, he saw Goering, whom he had often met at Berlin parties. Goering was wearing high boots, riding trousers and the brown shirt of the Storm Troopers, or S.A. Around his neck was a ribbon with the Pour le Mérite order for bravery. Next to him was Diels. Goering came up to Ripper and said: "Well, well, Baron. You aren't looking your usual elegant self. I understand you've been playing little games with us. Well, well. We know how to take care of you." He beamed, turned and departed.

That night Ripper was loaded into a truck and taken to the site of an old brewery on which the Oranienburg concentration camp had just been erected. As each prisoner stepped out of the van he was addressed as "Swine" and struck on the face with a whip. Then they were all conducted to cells which were, at least, no longer solitary.

From Oranienburg Ripper was allowed to send censored letters to his mother, although all efforts to establish direct contact with the Austrian Minister in Berlin failed. He wrote to the old baroness on April 13, 1934: "In the endless loneliness and fatigue of my cell I find I am surrounded with broken toys. I am surrounded with memories. All the months of my life which I have squandered are like a procession of ghosts which close in on me in my present ineffectuality. But it is good also to experience *this*. Nothing that a man experiences fully and completely and is conscious of can be in vain. Therefore do not worry about me, I will remain strong no matter what. I am still beginning my life and will realize someday that I have not lived in vain. When I walk in the courtyard, I think of our summer walks. The best of life lies in good memories. And I am happy. Be happy also."

Shortly afterward the camp commandant sent for him and said he had seen a few sketches Ripper had made on scraps of paper. These were pictures of prisoners to be given to their relatives when they paid the permitted monthly visits. The commandant was impressed with Ripper's talent. Since, like all Nazi officials, he wanted a large, splashy portrait of the Fuehrer, he assigned Ripper to the job and told him he could go to the nearest art store under guard and purchase all necessary materials.

For a month Ripper worked on this ludicrous task in a third-floor cell turned into his special studio. The portrait was knee-length, based on a photograph in which Hitler was giving the outstretched Nazi salute. Each day the commandant visited the studio to make comments. "That is not quite right," he would say. "The eyes should be powerful eyes, eyes of steel. But there should also be an expression of gentleness. The Fuehrer is a mild and gentle person with a big heart. You have not yet got the proper expression."

During his shopping tours for paints and brushes and during his deliberately long hours of portraiture, Ripper began to evolve an escape plan. It was, he decided, necessary to get a letter to the Austrian Minister. But no letters, except carefully excised ones to his mother, were allowed, and he could not tell whether his mother, living a country life in Salzburg, had the wit to realize that his plight was unknown to the Vienna Government.

Camp orders permitted that only direct relatives could visit prisoners. However, fiancées were included in the category of "direct relatives." Since his own wife, Mops, with whom he was now on bad terms, whose address he no longer knew, was, he feared, probably in prison, he had to invent a girl friend. He discussed this with his cellmates. One of them promised to arrange for a "fiancée" from among the friends of his own wife, after the next visitors' day. Furthermore, a code would be prepared to send on her name and address in advance.

Ripper then studied the exact color of the tin cups used by the Oranienburg inmates and purchased the necessary paints next time he went shopping for his Hitler portrait. He painted one side of a piece of paper the precise metallic shade. When it was dry, he wrote a message to the Austrian Minister on the other side, telling him where he was imprisoned.

A cousin of a fellow inmate's wife, a girl named Gretchen Panke, agreed to serve as "fiancée" and messenger. This news was conveyed in cipher and Ripper then asked for permission to have her call. The Oranienburg officials objected that, according to their records, he was married. Ripper explained he had broken off with his wife and hoped to wed Fräulein Panke as soon as he was released. Her visit was approved.

On the next visitors' day, wearing a scarf as identification for the fiancée he had never seen, Ripper joined the line waiting for relatives. They all met in a bare room across a large table with a Storm Trooper at each end. A wall ran from the bottom of the table to the floor so nothing could be passed beneath it. No one was permitted to pass across the top anything that was not first inspected and approved. However, the visitors were allowed to drink coffee provided by the prisoners. This came from their canteen together with a number of metal cups. Both visitors and prisoners had to serve themselves from large pots in the center of the table.

Ripper said to Miss Panke, who had greeted him with an affectionate kiss as soon as she saw the scarf: "Darling, I think your cup is dirty. You had better wipe it out." He had carefully folded inside it, tin-painted side out, his letter to the Austrian minister. Miss Panke showed the cup to the inspecting guard, who saw nothing suspicious. Then she took out a large handkerchief, scoured it, snatching up the message, and filled it with coffee. A week later, to his mild surprise, Ripper was given a brief official memorandum from the Austrian legation: "We have been informed you are being held in Oranienburg concentration camp. The legation will take all necessary steps to assist you."

Not long afterward Ripper was walking across the Oranienburg courtyard toward a storeroom when he saw a car with diplomatic plates and the Austrian flag parked at the gate. Beside it was one of the legation secretaries talking to the camp commandant. The commandant saw Ripper stop and stare, so he yelled to him: "Get along. Get along on your way." Ripper trudged on to the storeroom, never looking back. The following day he was given his own clothes, told to change and driven off in a Black Maria to Columbia House. There he was escorted to Diels' headquarters.

The Gestapo chief, Himmler's predecessor, asked him with great courtesy to sit down and offered a cigarette which Ripper refused. Then Diels said: "I wanted to talk to you because I am afraid some terrible mistake has been made here and I wish to apologize for the carelessness of some of my assistants."

Ripper stared bleakly back. "I shall remember their carelessness—and yours," he replied.

Diels was an extremely ambitious young bureaucrat. He had married the daughter of a wealthy industrialist and had served as a Nazi spy within the civil service before Hitler seized power. His reward had been appointment as Gestapo chief.

Diels smiled, only with his lips, and added: "I have one last word, mon cher Baron. When you get to Austria, or wherever you go, remember that the arm of the Gestapo can reach across our borders whenever it is necessary and wherever it is desired. So take my advice. Keep your mouth shut."

Ripper said nothing; he turned his back and departed. First he returned to his pension and discovered from his landlady that the police had told her he had left Germany because he was heavily in debt. When he went to his legation, he was informed that the Nazis had ordered him to leave the country within three days.

The Austrian Minister had heard nothing of Ripper's whereabouts until he received the strange note with silvery paint on one side. However, the old baroness had suspected something was wrong even before she received her son's first letter and had asked Vienna to make official inquiries of the German authorities. Apparently, she never knew just which camp he was in as the date and place of origin were excised from his mail. The police had told the Minister Ripper had run away from bankruptcy proceedings and they had no idea where he was.

Nevertheless, his mother persevered. The Austrians had arrested a certain Captain Leopold, a Nazi agent in Vienna, and they held him as a surety against Ripper's life. A quiet deal was made to exchange the two men.

Next day Ripper took a train to Holland. Later he recalled: "I didn't know then that I would not set foot on German soil again for more than a decade and that when I did I would be wearing the uniform of a country I had not yet even visited."

In Amsterdam he wrote a series of anti-Nazi articles which were widely reprinted and created a sensation. Afterward he went to Paris, where the Gestapo speedily denounced him to the authorities as a deserter from the Foreign Legion. André Malraux, a friend of his and influential as a renowned writer, intervened for Ripper so he wasn't drafted back to Sidi-el-Hani. Instead he fled to Majorca, which had become for him a haven of peace.

During the spring of 1935, that incredible Majorcan spring which comes in two waves, first blossoming fruit trees, pink and white above the green of young wheat, and then the blaze of yellow, ochre, pink and mauve, Ripper began a series of sardonic drawings on the hideous brutality of Nazi Germany. One sketch showed Hitler playing an organ attached to a Catherine wheel from which were strung agonized victims.

When he had completed this series he arranged an exhibit in London under the title *Ecrasez l'Infame*. Ribbentrop, at that time German Ambassador to the Court of St. James's, demanded that the show be closed or, at the very least, that the drawing of Hitler and his victims be removed as offensive to a head of state. The British politely refused.

However, Diels showed his extraterritorial talents. He could not, in England, denounce a man for desertion from the Foreign Legion. But Ripper had left the drawings at a print shop to be photographed and published in book form. These were mysteriously stolen and, despite a large reward for their recovery posted by the printer, they were never retrieved. Ripper later discovered that the man living in the hotel room next to his, registered as a Belgian but often heard speaking German, had left London the day after the sketches were taken to the printer.

Determined not to be thwarted in his fight against the

Nazis, Ripper spent months learning how to etch directly on copper plates and slowly repeated the entire series. These were eventually published in a limited edition and also displayed at a New York showing.

An event now occurred which enabled Ripper to kill Nazis rather than merely lampoon them. In 1936 the Spanish Civil War broke out and Hitler and Mussolini sent troops to the aid of General Franco. Today it is customary, victimized as we are by the lies of history, to consider that only Russia and the Communists came to help Spain's tottering republic. But such was far from the case. Many a good liberal shed his blood on the arid plateau of Castile.

Ripper was that strange phenomenon of our time, the artist *engagé* who, like Koestler or Malraux, wished to be part of events and not just to describe them. As a painter he had already pilloried the men and system he detested; but now, as a soldier, he wanted to fight and destroy them. So he enlisted in the final, drawn-out, intermittent battle of his life, a battle that never ended.

Just before the French Government joined in the paralytic policy of nonintervention, Ripper volunteered as an aerial machine-gunner in the republican forces. He was shot up and, in the hospital, discovered he had twenty-one shrapnel fragments in his legs and back. Invalided out, he was evacuated and finally decided to journey to the United States. (This episode as a soldier for the Republic, incidentally, was to worry him years later when he foolishly decided to settle in Franco Spain.)

In February, 1938, Ripper boarded a ship for New York.

He was intrigued by this new world, so remote from fever-
ish Europe. After selling some of his drawings he was
awarded a fellowship at Yaddo, the institute for young artists set up near Saratoga by the estate of George Foster
Peabody. Later he rented a small room in Greenwich Village and still later, for $50 a month, took over a barn-studio
in Connecticut. He furnished this, settled down, painted,
cooked lavish meals for himself and began a new tranquil
life. He fell in love and confided happily to his diary: "It's
a funny thing how it affects a man, the kind of woman he
sleeps with. A stranger in a new country will always be a
stranger until he falls in love with—and his love is recipro-
cated by—a woman of that country."

Immediately after Pearl Harbor he tried to volunteer in
the U.S. Army. He wished to feel part of this new land,
to serve it. However, he was rejected as a foreigner. Five
months later he was drafted. The medical examiner at first
refused to pass him because of his bad eye and the suspicion
of a heart murmur. Ripper argued: "What's the difference?
I can shoot with one eye. I've been shooting all my life. I've
served in the French and in the Spanish Army and I've done
very well with one eye. And my heart is fine." He showed
his twenty-three wound scars, so the doctor smiled and said:
"O.K., the hell with you. If you're that eager, it's all right
with me. But limited service only. I won't take the respon-
sibility for passing you into general service."

After basic training, which seemed to him odd and childish, he was attached to the special corps of painters whose
assignment was to record the exploits of American fighting
men. Almost eighteen months after the U.S. entered the

war he was flown in slow hops, with the lowest transport priority, to Africa.

Ripper's career in the United States Army was, to say the least, unusual; the artist-warrior who ended as a warrior-artist. Here was a middle-aged man, already thirty-eight when he went overseas as a technical sergeant, a man with immense fighting experience as compared to most other American N.C.O.'s, who were young enough to be his sons; a painter who had so often marched off to war and yet, this time, uniformed as a soldier, beginning his war with the assignment only to paint what he saw. He started in the North African Theatre in 1943 as a combat artist with the Corps of Army Engineers.

He enjoyed this mildly. He made innumerable sketches and some paintings of air bases in Algeria and Tunisia, taking particular delight in Luftwaffe strafing and bombing raids that gave action to his work. He was fascinated by the bright light and pastel shades of the southern Mediterranean shore. But he was impatient. What he wanted to do was kill Fascists, not immortalize their bodies with his brush.

At the end of the year he had himself transferred, still with noncommissioned rank, to the 34th Division, then stationed at Oran, near the border of Spanish Morocco, preparing for the invasion of Italy. Because he was bilingual he was put in an intelligence team to interrogate German prisoners. He took part in the Salerno landing and, as we advanced northward in Italy, wangled his way to a front-line job with the 168th Infantry Regiment.

On January 1, 1944, after being severely wounded on a

raiding operation, he was commissioned a second lieutenant. Eight months later he was promoted to first lieutenant
and ended the war as a captain, by then formally transferred
to O.S.S. as a parachutist agent ordered to help partisans in
his native Austria and often working in mufti as a spy.

It was during the cruel campaign in Italy that Rip earned
for himself a flamboyant name as a fighting man. Despite
his low rank he was widely known, even among senior
generals. General Lucian Truscott often called him "the
bravest man I've ever seen." General "Doc" Ryder, commanding the 34th Division, made a point of inviting him
around to drink and talk of war, this middle-aged artist who
gained fame and respect as a killer, who delighted in teasing
G.I.'s in their front-line foxholes by pretending to be a
"Kraut"—a dangerous game, that.

How does one describe the arduous Italian campaign, the
unprecedentedly cold winter, the frozen mud between the
Volturno and Rapido rivers where so much desperate fighting took place in the constricted valleys between sharp rows
of mountains? And when the thaws came, cold and marrow-
chilling, the ever-more-numerous cemetery mounds would
sink into the disintegrating ground while superstitious peasant grave diggers threw away their spades and fled in terror
from the moving graves.

This was a battle where machines had little value. Tank
commanders would curse and say: "I'd trade each vehicle
I've got for mules." Every evening the Graves Registration
Service would load their own mules and donkeys with the
corpses they picked up on hillsides and brought down to
pile in rows for identification and burial.

There were gloom, cold, grayness, sleet. And up around Cassino the bodies rotted in the narrow lowland of Purple Heart Valley, sprawled amid the letters from home and love notes soldiers always carry with them and, seemingly, always spill in final agony; the bodies lying among the mine fields, their throats eaten out by ravening village dogs deserted by their masters. And, intermittently, the whistling of that marvelous German gun, the eighty-eight, and the moan and crumping noise of multiple rockets, the *Nebelwerfer* or, as we used to call them, "screaming meemies."

Right in front of St. Benedict's massive abbey, situated on a hilltop, there was the most splendid deadly panorama war could have: a great stadium of death. All around, on the heights, sworn enemies could see the killing taking place. The Gurkhas, cut off in everyone's full view on that cynically named peak, Hangman's Hill, scuttled about for packets of ammunition, food and water every time our planes dove over them to drop the varicolored parachutes with which, for days, they were supplied. And then the night those Gurkhas opened their attack upon the monastery, creeping along with all the silence of Asia until a loud scream: "*Ayo Gurkhali, kukri nikali*, here come the Gurkhas, clasping their knives." They came, wielding their little curved butcher blades, scrambling up to the walls as the Nazis mowed them down in sheets of Schmeisser fire. And, again, the night when the French took over a sector from the British and the same little Gurkhas, sitting by log flames behind an olive grove, only their teeth and the whites of their eyes showing, watched the big Moroccan *goums* move in with quiet confidence, the men of the Himalayas and the men of the Atlas range regarding each other askance with curious admiration, knowing each other as mountain men and fighters who preferred the knife.

Ripper kept a diary on and off throughout the war, a small leather-bound volume which I now have, slightly worn at the edges and sweat stained. In it one can glimpse the sensitivity of the artist hidden behind the tough, bellicose exterior of the warrior and the rough, sardonic humor that gave rise to so many legends of The Ripper.

After he was wounded, south of the Rapido, having been shot twice in the right hand, once in the left arm, once in the shoulder and once in the face (scarring the upper lip and nose base), he was taken to the 15th Evacuation Hospital. There, on November 26, 1943, as he lay slowly but optimistically recovering, he wrote in this journal:

"It's a curious thing when one gets wounded, though I have experienced it before. It's new every time. The nearness of death is like an icy draft around one. First you don't feel anything—then you are surprised at being alive and feel down your body to find out how much of it is there. Then you get goddamn mad at yourself—at least I did this time —that the other guy got the better of you, was faster on the trigger than yourself."

A few days later, as he lay in bed with nothing to do but think, he wrote rather awkwardly (because of his wounded hand): "The three things I fear most: get taken prisoner by the Nazis, lose my left eye [the good one] or have my right hand disabled [the one with which he painted].

"Funny how someone who is so attracted by women, like I am, and to whom sex is a very important part of life, can live so quietly in this world of men that is an army. There is a sadness in being a man, but it's a proud thing too."

A fortnight later, when all his wounds except those on the hand had fairly well healed, half his right index finger was amputated. Rip confided to his diary: "It hurt like hell afterward." He then continued: "How utterly senseless and cruel war is. And with these visions, a black fear to go out again at night, where death might be at any step in the darkness.

"And still, somehow I feel, when the time comes again, I shall go out again. It isn't what they call heroism. It's acceptance of fate, a submission unto the greater thing, the necessity.

"And I'll go out first again; something pushes me to do so. It's a proud thing too, being a man. But it's also an immense pity for the others; that burning love for human beings which has driven me all these years, made me outlive Nazi prisons and all their horrors, without losing my mind.

"There can be peace only when these things, the source of all today's sufferings, are stamped out forever. That is peace for me.

"And all the while the desperate longing to be back in my studio and paint, peaceful and quiet, and all the struggle directed to create instead of to destroy and kill."

It is odd, today, to read these confessions of a man regarded as a legendary killer by thousands of G.I.'s in that desperate mountainous battlefield between Naples and the Gustav Line where Hitler's paratroopers made their gallant and ferocious stand. As he was recovering from the amputation of part of his finger, Rip scrawled painfully:

"I've often wondered what it is that makes men go into battle and risk their lives, which is their all. It would be ridiculous to pretend that we all are not full of fear—because we are. And it is not heroism or patriotism or any of the so-called higher feelings that makes us go, again and again, with our hearts beating.

"Somehow, when things move fast, one forgets a little bit that the next bullet might have one's number on it. But when the fight goes slow and every shell singing by sings of death, we are very conscious of having only one life to live and how precious it is.

"And how stupid it is to get killed, to shoot at each other and to destroy that poor little life, which at times has been and can be so pleasant. It is not fatalism either, that makes us go, although many will pretend that's what it is.

"What it is, I am sure, simply is pressure of society. That pressure is greater than the fear of bullets or shells or mines. It's a spiritual fear and therefore stronger than the other, the physical fear."

Rip was aware of the universality of his anguish, of the torment suffered by other, less sensitive souls. He wrote: "All these boys here, like myself, who have been wounded, lightly or seriously, have felt that cold breath of death on our cheeks—and when we go back we shall be more frightened than we were the first time. But we all go back, because there is nothing else to do.

"What we call heroism—or heroic acts—is, I believe, mostly the result of a man's stronger consciousness of what his pals, his officers, his men—or even his girl at home—think of him, stronger than is his fear of shells.

"Many of the things I have done, I know today, have been done for the above reasons. But, somehow, with me it is also a question of pride, the continuous necessity to—so to speak—prove myself to myself. To act the things—or rather to prove by my deeds the words I have spoken, the ideas I believe in."

There is the quality of the man, the man reputed a fearless desperado.

As soon as Rip became ambulatory, he was permitted to stroll around Caserta, the town where the hospital was situated. He used to sit in a little bar drinking white wine and watching the smoke from Vesuvius spiral upward into the sky. Vesuvius was almost as active that winter as the battlefield itself.

The regiment to which he had attached himself, the 168th, at that time took heavy casualties in four days of fighting near Monte Pontano. Rip wrote: "An awful lot—they sure are coming in here these last three days. Some just lie quiet on their stretchers and some moan softly in that curious faint voice of people talking to themselves. They just can't help it. Their bodies are the instrument of living and that instrument doesn't function the way they are used to."

When he was well enough, he went off with some other officers to Pompeii. He wrote afterward: "It was a very enjoyable afternoon. We first ate lunch at a little restaurant with the accompaniment of a small orchestra with a terrible old tenor. And we drank a lot of cognac. Then we went to the excavations and spent hours walking along the streets and looking into the houses.

"It is amazing how fresh and vivid that place is. It seems to one that people must have lived there yesterday and not 2,000 years ago. Maybe that comes from being so used to destroyed towns, from going through ruins where people did live a few days before."

He had an excellent Christmas, describing it as: "Very fine, very G.I. I got drunk for three days, got laid by a nice girl and was with a lot of swell guys and some of my old friends. And now back to work."

In January, 1944, Ripper was ordered to report at 34th Division headquarters, where he ran into his old friend General Ryder. Ryder had high respect for him. Before he was wounded, Rip had been involved in some detective work that followed an American discovery of ghastly Nazi brutalities near Caiazzo.

When the Americans entered the woods near the village of San Giovanni they found the bodies of four girls, all under twenty, naked. They had been raped and then kicked to death. Rip, as a prisoner-of-war interrogator, was assigned to find out who were the criminals. He determinedly broke down a Nazi lieutenant and sergeant among the prisoners; they confessed. Ryder was pleased when he heard about this. He called Ripper in, grinned at him and said: "Well, I hear you finally got some back at those bastards for what they did to you."

Rip was attached as an intelligence officer to the 109th Engineers. He was pleased with this assignment because it allowed him time to sketch and paint. He confided to himself: "It's a lovely thing. And for my 38 years, I am not doing so badly. I was worried how I would be able to stand the strain physically, but I find it's okay."

Immediately he began to seek new perils. His diary recalls: "I went up the side of a hill to find out what the situation was. On the way, crawling on my belly because of mortar fire, I stopped at a dugout and asked an officer of the chemical mortars which was the way. Because of my accent and my German field glasses he suspected me as a German spy or something. I had a few very uncomfortable minutes."

While fighting he began a large painting of the Cassino battle. He used to go around the foxholes sketching dead soldiers. On January 30, 1944, he wrote: "Yesterday was my 39th birthday. I am getting to be an old bird. But I feel as young as can be."

Despite his pleasure at sketching and painting again, Ripper wanted to resume front-line action. But Ryder's chief of intelligence said to him: "If I let you go, you will be out on patrols right away and getting shot up again. Then I will get the blame. The War Department doesn't want you to fight. It wants you to paint. So get the hell out of here."

Rip commented in his journal: "Little does he know. That very same morning I tried to get into Cassino and got sniped down in a house." Cassino at that time was three-quarters occupied by the Germans and one quarter by the Allies.

Ripper wrote: "I made a sketch from there and I was lucky I got out. It seems silly to expose oneself like that to make a drawing. But to me it is necessary to get there when they fight. I want the atmosphere of the fight. I want the atmosphere of men's anxiety and fear, that exposure to death which leaves a deep stamp on human faces."

From the point of view of artist or observer Cassino was unique in World War II: a holocaust concentrated on a single little mountain town. When the bombing and shelling were over, Cassino bore a striking resemblance to the surface of the moon. One could creep along the cliff path beneath lowering Monte Cairo and suddenly, upon the very outskirts, great tanks like beetles would spit sheets of fire. Patrols inched gingerly from room to room in what had once been houses.

The hillsides were littered with the pathetic, tiny shoes of Hawaiian *nisei*, who fought so determinedly to prove their patriotism and suffered so cruelly from the frostbite of the Apennines. One day a German officer, heading a line of prisoners filing to the rear, exclaimed to the American lieutenant leading them: "But those replacements coming up, they're Japanese." "Sure," said his captor. "Didn't you know they were on our side? Or do you believe everything Goebbels tells you?"

When he got back from that battle, Ripper was given two days' leave in Naples. He picked up a girl and took her home. He reflected on this experience: "It is a strange thing to lie in bed with a strange woman, in strange foreign rooms, cold and empty mostly, where very often you look out on wrecked houses, their sides torn open and their entrails of chairs and tables, dressers and broken mirrors, hanging out into the street. You look at them, your head on a pillow, the soft curve of the young woman's breasts close to your eyes."

May came. The Fifth Army finally broke through the Cassino gap and Ripper found: "Now that it's warm, it's a lot easier to fight, less grim. Nature, the foliage of the trees and the lovely, lush vegetation provide wonderful cover for the men who creep up on each other to kill. And on the other hand, the contrast becomes grimmer, more terrible. There are places around Cassino and on the beachhead [Anzio] where every tree is torn, where the earth is plowed by hundreds of shells, and instead of grain, steel is strewn all over."

He often reflected on the meaning of death and the curious sensation of killing. He had fought already in two wars, against the mountainous Druse tribes in the Levant and against the Fascist forces in Spain, but he had never shot a man at close range and seen him fall dead before him. He learned this art in Italy.

Later on he told Avi, his second wife: "I still wake up and see that one, the first. I don't even know if he was a Nazi. He was a young fellow. I didn't have time to hate him. I shot from the hip and he fell right at my feet. We were on patrol, you know.

"He kept looking into my eyes. That upset me. It still upsets me. He really seemed such a sympathetic type. He was too young to have known the Gestapo men who tortured me. But maybe he tortured others? Do you think so?

"It's a funny thing about blood. When you spill it once, you find it easier afterwards. I found it easier, both with a gun and with a knife. You do it because you have to do it. But it isn't natural. In the end it gives you ulcers."

In the spring of 1944, before Rome's liberation, Ripper

met a cousin of his mother's, from the English branch of
the Salis family, who was serving as a British intelligence
colonel in a special branch called A-Force. The job of
A-Force was to help Allied prisoners in Axis territory escape
and also to add to the general espionage picture.

The English colonel had heard of Ripper's exploits and
asked if he would undertake an assignment for A-Force.
When Rip agreed, he was temporarily detached from the
34th Division and, after an extensive briefing, was taken
by submarine to the Italian coast north of Rome, where
he disembarked in a small rubber dinghy. He was wearing
a seminary priest's red cassock and bore papers attesting
that he was a student at the Collegium Germanicum, the
Vatican's German academy for priests.

Ripper had boarded the submarine with a British Navy
duffel coat over his uniform and, once aboard, changed into
clerical robes. Even for a veteran adventurer this was an odd
experience: the uncanny silence of a submerged vessel skirt-
ing the desperate and embattled Anzio beachhead, the taci-
turn crew and humming of engines dulled by the pressure
that encompassed them, the confinement, the pale sailors,
the clipped, soft English voices, and, weirdest of all, that
gaudy priestly costume.

When they surfaced off the point of rendezvous, there
was a brief whispered conversation on deck: "The password
is Giudita. The answer must be Amore. When you get used
to the dark you will see a low rocky shore, a clump of trees.
In a small cove below the clump a man will be waiting for
you. Good luck."

He was helped into the frail dinghy and shoved off. The

submarine disappeared behind him with a slight gurgling
noise. It was a pitch-black night so, used as he was to fighting in the mountains, Ripper sat back for several minutes
with his eyes closed. When he at last could see something
he paddled to the coast.

He was met by two Italian partisans. Passwords were
murmured and they escorted him to a highway, where they
waited impatiently for dawn. There was no regular transportation but it was then the custom for trucks to serve as
buses for hitchhikers. The leading partisan flagged down a
camion of vegetables and all three climbed in. They were
stopped twice, once by a squad of Mussolini's soldiers and
once by a German roadblock, but their papers were found
in order after a cursory glance.

The Rome of that spring, 1944, was a dying capital,
haughtily disdainful of the changes taking place as Rome
has always been haughtily disdainful. The grandeur of Fascist dreams was dissolving in decay. Mussolini had with-
drawn northward and it was Hitler's troops who rounded
up hostages after each partisan shooting, marched them
through the night to catacombs, machine-gunned them and
dynamited the entrances to these caves of death.

Only a few miles distant, between the pleasant beach
resorts of Anzio and Nettuno, the Nazis sought desperately
and vainly to drive the Allies from their beachhead into
the sea. And each night in the blackout the Romans peered
from their balconies and rooftops to watch the flickering
display of fireworks.

All the whores of Italy had gathered in eager anticipation
of the entry of rich Americans and comely English lads.

And in the Vatican preparations were being made to move out Allied refugees and replace them with Axis fugitives seeking shelter in the bosom of an impartial church. There were movement, agitation, poverty and hope; and always the heavy-handed terror of the trigger-happy Nazis with their Schmeissers. And imagine in all this fetid atmosphere an American officer of Austrian descent, dressed in the garb of a German priest and spying for the British.

Ripper was taken to the home of a British agent in the Trastevere district. He spent several days there, in radio contact with A-Force headquarters to the south, before undertaking his special assignment. This was the rather audacious venture of contacting still another cousin of his and the A-Force colonel's, an Austrian Salis with high rank in the Abwehr, German military intelligence, at Field Marshal Kesselring's headquarters. He sent a message to this man under his real name, recalling their relationship, claiming to be a seminary student and asking if they could meet.

The Austrian officer received him with curiosity. After they had talked for some time about mutual relatives, about Rome and about the course of the war, Ripper sought information on the situation in Austria. A-Force had informed him that this cousin, serving the enemy, was in fact an anti-Nazi and an Austrian nationalist. Such turned out to be the truth and the two men became increasingly candid. Only then did Ripper disclose his official identity and mention their cousin in A-Force. The Austrian was startled and worried but not entirely surprised. He told Rip he would not betray him but that he had better leave Rome as soon as possible. The Nazis were already suspicious of the Abwehr, which was headed by Admiral Canaris. (Canaris was to be executed that summer for participation in the July 20th plot to assassinate Hitler.)

Before leaving, Ripper asked whether there were many anti-Nazis in Austria. The answer was yes. "However," said his cousin, "you will never be able to form a resistance movement because there are no men. Everyone is at the front. Any able-bodied man spotted by the police is immediately arrested and held unless he can produce exceptionally good reasons for not being in uniform. I know, in my heart, that the war is already over and terrible things are coming. I believe you when you say you'd like to help our country. But I also believe this is not possible. Now give my compliments to our English colonel and leave. Please don't come back and please get out of Rome."

Ripper spent a few more days with the British agent gathering information about prisoners, most of whom were hidden in near-by monasteries. He was then instructed by radio to return to headquarters. Italian partisans smuggled him out, gave him peasant's clothing near the Allied lines and helped him across a mountain trail to safety.

That summer, after Rome's liberation, Ripper settled in an apartment with the English writer Christopher Sykes, a captain in the Coldstream Guards, and continued to work with A-Force. He established relations with some Austrian diplomats and refugees at the Vatican and explored the possibilities of developing a partisan network and prisoner-escape route in south Austria. In between, he lived a most luxurious life in Sykes' requisitioned flat with servants, batmen, two automobiles and a charming Roman war widow. He found this delightful and interesting but remote from combat.

He wrote in his diary: "I want to take a parachute course and a short course in demolitions, ciphers, etc. Then I want to go up there, along the Austrian-Slovenian border, at the beginning of October and use that territory as a base of operations and of penetration."

To fulfill this ambition he was transferred to O.S.S., the American intelligence agency, and sent to the jump school at Gioia del Colle, where he passed the parachute course by the somewhat novel methods earlier described. Then he was summoned to main headquarters in Caserta and given the fake papers and cover name of Carl Reber.

In Bari, take-off point for the Balkan Air Force which dispatched and supplied guerrilla agents, he waited to begin his first mission—to the Pohorje Mountains in northern Yugoslavia, near the Austrian frontier. At the last minute this operation was canceled, after he had happily noted in his diary: "At last, tonight, came the go-ahead signal. So with a pocket full of gold and money and a lovely new Marlin sub-machine gun, I am off tomorrow morning. The plan looks good; so let's hope for the best! Off to the races!"

The subsequent two operations were also washed out. Each time the plane took off but, because of weather conditions, had to turn back. Finally, in December, 1944, Ripper was dropped in a region near Maribor, Yugoslavia, identified on German maps as the Bechter Gebirge. His orders were to proceed northward on his own into the Austrian area around Klagenfurt, to establish an escape route and, if possible, help organize the flight of Allied soldiers held in prisoner-of-war camps along the Drava River valley.

It was a moonlit winter night when he bailed out of his aircraft. Below him he could see a great white mountaintop of snow surrounded by pine forests. Later he recalled the sensation of floating down: "The moon illuminated the landscape just enough to make out the crags, the rocks, the snow, patches of Alpine grass, and the heavily timbered ring around this; lovely silvery light and dead quiet."

On the edge of the trees he found a large brigade head-quarters of Tito's Partisan army. They had a neat encampment, well camouflaged. Although the Germans knew they were there, they left them alone as too strong to tackle on unfavorable terrain. The Yugoslav commander greeted Ripper and the radio technician who had been dropped with him. But when he discovered Rip's fluent German, he became suspicious and reserved. The brigade contained several Austrian deserters and prisoners. They had been allowed to volunteer but were not permitted weapons except in action and were kept under perceptible watch.

Ripper stayed with the Partisans a week and then, dressed in civilian clothes, moved on to Klagenfurt. He remained there ten days and was horrified at how bad the situation was. It was indeed true that there were no young men left. The entire male population had been drafted for emergency service by the collapsing Nazi regime.

Consequently, Ripper returned to the Partisan brigade near Maribor and, with two of their soldiers as guides, worked his way southward to a small airstrip. Here he was picked up by a Piper Cub from the Balkan Air Force and flown to a larger field, whence a bomber took him back to Italy.

He spent the next two weeks conferring with O.S.S. officials in Rome. He argued that, despite the difficult situation he had found, it was necessary to make an effort to encourage serious Austrian resistance. A resistance movement would be able to help form a postwar government. Finally, he gained his point. It was at first decided to send him to Switzerland with fake documents as a U.S. consular official but the State Department disapproved. So he was parachuted once again in March, 1945, some weeks before V-E day.

The situation in his native land was especially complex. In a sense an unwilling enemy, Austria had been absorbed by Hitler's *Anschluss* six years before but it scarcely protested at the time and furnished the Fuehrer some of his ablest troops. Yet the disillusionment, even among Austrian Nazis, had been keen.

Now this little country, so soon to become a killing ground, looked with terror to the approaching Slavic armies, Russians from the east and Yugoslav Partisans from the south. To atavistic dread was added the hatred of Communism so native to a devoutly Catholic nation.

There was a craving for change, an eagerness to shed the shackles imposed on it as Hitler's Ostmark, but intense anxiety about the future. And all the young men of Austria were fighting in the sandy Prussian plains, the Carpathian foothills and the mountains of north Italy, far from their menaced homes.

Ripper landed in south Austria and, carrying his papers, spare clothes, a map and radio transmitter in a tightly bound waterproof sack, swam a stream to a designated rendezvous. There he was met by two peasants, who guided him across a woods and through the nervous German lines to the mansion of an Austrian nationalist known to Allied agents. This man, a country aristocrat, had been wounded in Russia while fighting as a conscripted German officer.

Ripper stayed with him several days. He passed the time wandering about his host's hunting preserve with the old gamekeeper, maintaining radio contact with O.S.S. through brief transmissions from continually changing points, and endlessly arguing politics. With his host and the gamekeeper he surveyed the possibilities of forming cadres for a national resistance movement. But, although they were enthusiastic, there weren't any men available to join.

Therefore Ripper decided to move to Klagenfurt and see if he could do better in a city. He had a set of carefully forged papers under the name of an Austrian draftsman, and, in clothes provided by the aristocrat, went to the nearest town to take a train. His luck, however, was against him.

During those desperate last days the Gestapo had initiated the custom of suddenly descending on railway stations and rounding up everyone to check their papers. Ripper seemed entirely too healthy so, despite the excellence of his documents, he was taken to local police headquarters. The official in charge placed a telephone call to the factory at

Linz, in upper Austria, where the "draftsman" said he was employed on special projects, exempt from military service.

Ripper, like all Allied agents, was equipped with a cyanide pill for suicide in case of capture. This was not only to elude Nazi savagery but also to prevent the yielding of secrets to devices such as truth drugs like scopolamine. The cyanide was encased in a fragile capsule. When this was slipped into the mouth, it could easily be crushed with the teeth.

As soon as the official placed his call, Rip, sitting lumpishly on a wooden bench and protesting at the waste of time, managed to work the pill out from the lapel of his jacket, where he had secreted it, and to slip it between his lips while covering a cough. Then, although he was not a very religious man, he said a prayer and waited for death, ready to crush the cyanide capsule when he had to. He told me afterward: "No man, no' matter how brave, who has gone through torture once can be sure he'll stand up to it a second time. I knew, or I thought I knew, I couldn't."

Fortunately, however, there had been a particularly heavy American bomber raid that morning on the Austrian factory complex in the north. The principal telephone lines were down. So, while Ripper sat with his tongue pressing the poison capsule against his lower teeth, the Gestapo agent became increasingly impatient.

He kept telling the operator to connect him urgently as soon as the wires were functioning. But, in the meantime, his wife called twice to say: "We have a roast in the oven and it has already been cooked too long. You know how difficult it is to get meat these days. In heaven's name come

63

home now or it will spoil." In the end, greed overcame duty. The official inspected Rip's fabricated documents once more and dismissed him. Ripper spat the cyanide tablet into his hand and marched indignantly away.

When the Nazi forces surrendered after Hitler's death, Ripper was still in Austria, where he had managed to form a small underground movement. He rushed up to Salzburg to find his old mother, the Baroness Claire. While he was there, he spotted a strangely familiar face, that of a huge, scarred man who casually produced papers under the name of Berger. Rip was positive that, in fact, this was Otto Skorzeny, the remarkable Nazi commando chief who led a parachute raid that liberated Mussolini from his Allied captors, one of World War II's most dramatic feats. He had Skorzeny arrested. Unfortunately, a bumbling counter-intelligence officer later released him and he slipped away to Spain.

Years afterward, in Madrid's famous Horcher's restaurant, with its heavy, dark furnishings and heavy, rich cuisine, Ripper saw sitting at a nearby table an immense individual with a cicatrice. They nodded amiably and Skorzeny rose to join him. "May I sit down?" he asked. "You know, I remember you quite well."

"You certainly do," said Ripper. "It is too bad that circumstances kept me from returning to Salzburg in time to prevent your release. You must consider yourself fortunate here."

"Yes," said Skorzeny with a smile. "Perhaps more fortunate than you are."

Immediately after the war, when Ripper was demobilized, he returned to the United States and began painting again in his New England barn. He became strongly attracted to a tall, golden-haired California girl named Evelyn Leege. "Evi" to his Teutonic ear and accent became "Avi." As soon as divorce papers dissolved his marriage to Mops, following her release from Ravensbrück, he married for a second time.

From the start he told Avi: "Kid, there are only two ways of living—in the Ritz or on a bench in the park." He persuaded her to leave America and go off to start a new life in Pollensa, on the Spanish island of Majorca, where he had an eye on a property he had first seen years ago. "For God's sake," she argued, "why go there? You must be anathema to the Fascists. And anyway it's too remote." But he insisted. He insisted that an island was what he needed, that if it was remote in winter, in summer it was cosmopolitan, and that anyway he wanted to dwell among the purple, gold and amethyst cliffs he knew so well.

So, with his usual disdain for reality, Ripper decided to settle on the lotus-eating island which pertained not only to the last state professing the Fascism he had for so long fought, Spain, but which was a hidey-hole for many outstanding Nazis who escaped the vengeance of an Allied victory. He bought a lovely house, surrounded by garden and swimming pool, and furnished it with splendor.

One summer, when I was visiting him there, after a Lucullan dinner he himself had cooked, I asked him, sitting in his gentle garden, fragrant with the early night fragrance, why he of all people had returned to this piece of the world, this strange and stultifying land with its dour gendarmes and their varnished cardboard hats, this corrupt bureaucracy of which he already complained, and these evil Nazi neighbors, like Skorzeny and his refugee friends. Why not a Greek island, if he sought the Mediterranean?

He spoke of the beauty. He spoke of the benefits, to a painter, of this land of cockaigne. He spoke of the crumbling, even there in Spain, of what was left of Fascism. He spoke of the advantages of a foothold in the Old World into which he had, after all, been born. And he spoke of the gaiety, the parties and the yachts and frivolous women of nearby Formentor. And he added: "Why should I care about these final-vestige Fascists, these dodo birds? Although they are too stupid to recognize the facts of life, they are doomed. They hate me but I have contempt for them. I ignore them. They have outlived their time, my time."

How wrong he was. Perhaps they had outlived their time, but, in a sense, Ripper never inhabited his own. And a man, on the whole, is bound irrevocably to his time. If he chooses to violate contemporary rules in his way of life he is doomed.

Maybe Ripper knew all this—but he didn't care. By nature he was an independent and by doctrine, if anything, an anarchist. A democrat in theory, believing in the majority's right to lay down civilization's pattern, he chose to ignore that pattern, suspecting he might someday have to pay for this decision, suspecting and not caring.

In 1960, on the excuse that he wanted to nourish his creative mind with new ideas and, incidentally, purchase stones for his jeweled artifacts in the cabochon marts of

Asia, he took Avi off on a lengthy round-the-world tour, gaudy, spendthrift and delightful.

They arrived in Paris late that spring, minds bursting with experience and baggage bursting with strange purchases, Oriental patterns of workmanship and bags of gems to be fabricated into new designs. "My God," said Rip, "now I can really get to work. When I've finished up this lot I'll concentrate on painting. That's still the only thing I really want to do."

They were staying with us, and one day, sitting in the Ritz Bar where Avi jangled bracelets before the eyes of envious females and admiring males as she sipped champagne, I asked Ripper how on earth he planned to take this complicated batch of stuff across the frontiers of our technically hidebound and conventional world. How strange a question to pose to the man who had driven carloads of uninsured modern art to Vienna's first postwar exhibition, who had been an arms runner in warlord China, an aerial machine-gunner in Spain; who had outwitted Hitler's myrmidons and fought in the French Foreign Legion. "What's the problem?" he inquired. "I'll just take them."

So they took them. And one fine morning, he in his fire-engine-red sports car and she in an only slightly more conventional Mercedes, started off for Majorca bulging with weirdly-assorted possessions. On the border near Barcelona, from where the Balearic Islands ferry leaves, they were picked up by the Spanish customs. They had been denounced as "smugglers" by an anonymous "friend." (Was this an echo of Diels?) They argued that it is scarcely "smuggling" when you carry your goods openly and declare them for what they are. But this made little difference.

Avi wrote from Barcelona: "Please get out your reading-in-between-the-lines glasses because, chum, here you really have the totalitarian state at work. The phones of the consulate here, the Ritz (where we are staying), our lawyers: all are tapped. Letters are disappearing like straws. Others are obviously opened, as enclosures, mentioned enclosures, are always missing. On the island, where we are finally going tomorrow night, it will be worse.

"So now I will tell you what happened. I crossed the border with the usual formalities—and was arrested twenty minutes later mysteriously and held, being grilled for fourteen hours by a sadist, the agent in charge, who before he had even looked at anything in my possession said I was a professional smuggler of a large value of diamonds. What I had with me were my own clothes, stuff for the house, paints and canvas for Rip, and my jewel case of my own stuff.

"Incommunicado—and forced to sign false statements with no chance to call for help outside, let alone an interpreter. I was told that I had been denounced for this crime and, as you know, here you are guilty before proven innocent, with little chance of proving that because everything is rigged ahead of time.

"They picked up Rip on the same charge at the Ritz, whisked him under false pretenses to where I was—all illegal.

"The next day we got lawyers. And then we found out that in this incredible system here, if they evaluate the property they have seized which they consider contraband at a fantastic sum (they forgot about the diamonds fast and hardly even looked at my baggage), they can then get a fine which is five times the amount of evaluation. This goes like this—one third to the informer, one third to the flatfoot who mistreated me and one third to the State. So you see the picture.

"Two days later, having given our house and boat and two cars as guarantee, we left for Madrid passportless to see the embassy. The ambassador, whom we have known for some time, sent an informal protest, then a formal one, demanding return of passports and enough time to prepare our defense as well as a personal guarantee of our safety. The embassy is 100% behind us and very worked up.

"Result: the flatfoot who tried to terrorize me got a reprimand. The passports, under various pretenses and lies, will not be back until tomorrow. And we have a month's delay. The court of trial is pretty rigged. There is a new head man who will want a brilliant start and this flatfoot working day and night to make his career. Their careers are in the balance, so you can guess what's coming.

"God, Cy, what a mess. You were right about a Greek island. It certainly was wiser to think of living on a Greek island than on one in this country. It is too bad that this lovely country is a magnolia of sun, sherry, flamenco and bullfights—covering its drawbacks."

To this was appended a postscript: "To show you what that flatfoot is doing, he confiscated twelve lipsticks and six tubes of toothpaste saying I was trafficking in both, but handed me back a new toaster and steam iron. The whole thing is revolting."

As soon as we got this news I said to my wife: "I wonder what this will do to Ripper's heart." He had been complaining during that last visit: "I'm fifty-six now and I guess I'd better slow up. The doctor told me I have a leaky valve in the ventricle. But he gave me some pills and whenever I get a pain I take them. I've cut down a bit on my smoking" (said he as he opened a second pack) "and, as for drink, he told me it was a stimulant. Let's have another."

Avi had also confessed that she was worried. Rip was no longer young but seemed to consider himself indestructible. He often complained of pains in the arms and chest. After all, he bore twenty-seven wounds plus scars of torture. Twice he had fainted; but each time he insisted on getting out of bed, after taking a handful of pills, and going out to parties, all dolled up in dinner jacket with string tie and frilled shirt, just as if he were a twenty-five-year-old Fancy Dan.

And now, after a four-month tour which included every museum, historical monument and a majority of the night clubs on their global circuit, the pains and fatigue were worse. A quiet summer in Pollensa might at least be helpful; but not a session of fighting bureaucracy's strangling red tape.

The answer came all too soon.

I was in the United States when Rip died in 1960, on my way to the convention at Los Angeles where the Democratic party nominated Kennedy for the Presidency. First there was a brief cable from my wife with the cruel news. She flew right down to Majorca. Then there was a short dispatch published on the obituary page of *The New York Times*. And then I got a tragic letter from Avi. She wrote:

"I am so dazed myself. The whole story was bad enough but now it is horrible and our poor Rip, finally the victim of what he had fought against all his life.

"The excitement and gruesomeness of this hideous last month of his life was what his great heart could not take. We all know what we have lost. How he would like to know how we all loved him. He despaired so in this last month and worried so for me. . . .

"Rip came back from Madrid where he saw the U.S. chargé d'affaires and some Spanish friends who told him to go back and rest as this famous trial will be the beginning of September. He was so cheerful but dreadfully tired and looked very un-Ripperish.

"He kept taking those heart pills—as he did all month— and the next day promised me he would take a month's vacation. He did not know that the endless one had already been arranged.

"Friends came—our best Spanish friends who had just returned to the island and who helped me through the rest. We had dinner. He kept complaining that his arm ached and rubbing his chest. We went to bed. I woke up. I found his glasses and book and with some wild premonition of I don't know what started to look for him.

"He was dead when I found him, only neither the servants nor I knew it. The doctor finally came and then we called the Spanish friends.

"He was a great human being who never spared himself

or complained and the fifteen years I had with him were crazy, but it was living all right. He knew how to give—to everybody—except himself.

"We had such plans and now all that's left is the pieces.

"They even fussed over his burial place. I had his Catholic baptismal certificate, but he didn't confess in the local church, although he gave money, flowers, and helped the priests whenever they came around. Technicalities. Those inhumanities. Then, the doctor should have telephoned the priest to come right away. How should I know? I'm a Buddhist myself.

"So they shoved him into a box—it looks like a compartment of an icebox—in the Protestant part of the cemetery. You can imagine if this country is officially Catholic what that corner would look like.

"But for his memory as an American who did something for his country, I am going to buy a plot and make those other graves of his faith look like anthills.

"So there, Cy—our Rip."

My wife, Marina, arrived a few hours after Avi had finished this desolate letter. She wrote two days later: "I came here because Avi is in such an awful state, poor thing, and the nights seem endless to her. Remorse. Bitter regret. Looking back all the time on all the things she did or did not do which could have caused him pain and suffering. All this comes out in one sad ballad to which I can say nothing except to add my own tears and perhaps a kiss and a hand held tight.

"So we sit in the scented air of that garden, where every leaf is his, every branch, every stone, and which, with the total indifference of nature to the fates of her men, seems more beautiful and luscious than ever this summer.

"She found him in the garden, you know. He must have felt the need for air and gone out for a breath. She woke up later on, and finding the bed beside her empty, rushed out to look for him, and found him in the garden.

"She was alone in the house, but for the maids, and the doctor did not come for hours; and then he neglected to send for a priest with the result that poor Rip, although a Catholic, was buried without a priest in the Protestant patch where all infidels go.

"Naturally rumor is rampant. They are saying in the village that it was suicide or something strange. And they are even saying that the Guardia Civil opened the grave and found only bags of stones and that he is not dead but only hiding to avoid the trial.

"Avi does not know this, thank God. But she knows about the suicide rumor. The whole thing is so appalling. And of course I understand now that they were denounced as contrabandistas.

"Secret denunciations don't have to be proved. And it means that if the lawyer does not manage somehow to get a more lenient sentence she loses all her jewels, all her other things, and both cars.

"She is without a car now and you don't know what a sense of claustrophobia one gets tucked away in this place whose very beauty is heavy and strange. His presence is everywhere, in every bit of furniture, in every picture, even in the food and drink. Oh dear, how awful it all is.

"Your letters to her have just arrived and the obituaries

and I must say, in all the drama, we could not help laughing at what you said so admiringly—that he had fought on the loyalist side. That's *all* she needs just now to fix her up proper with the authorities."

To this my dear wife added the postscript: "Don't let's ever die except together."

A week later I received another letter in Los Angeles as the Democratic politicians were haggling away in airconditioned hotel rooms. It seemed so strange to hear these gruesome tales from a perfumed Mediterranean island. Marina wrote:

"I must say there is nothing worse than a bigoted, inbred, black Catholic village, and especially to a mad, wild, unconventional couple like the Rips. You can't imagine what the rumors are.

"Even a few days ago the police came to ask the carpenter who made the coffin if he had really put Rip's body into it or if it was stones and cement. All they had to do was to go to the cemetery which, God help me, smells so terrible that one could not get within thirty yards of where the coffin had been left.

"Too, too macabre. Imagine a priest who refuses to bury a man. Oh dear. And, of course, Avi in scarlet trousers and long earrings is not going to be an impressive widow either, although I must say she has not been out of the house once since he died."

And then, at the end of the sad, sad summer, a kind of postscript from Avi, sent from Switzerland, where she was staying with her sister, far away and oddly remote from the hideous scene of her tragedy. She said:

"Zurich is so splendidly comfortable and safe, in Gwen's delicious house. What a relief to be munching chocolate and discussing Rilke rather than which character can be bought, and which one would be bought and double-cross, or how much it would cost to hire somebody to have somebody have an accident. (Oh, no, not in a Catholic country.) So fed up with high drama and tricks, legends—but I guess if you're going to have it, you might as well have every bit of it, down to the last crumb, and not cheat yourself. . . .

"As the non-existent sun sets behind a curtain of howling rain and trees over all that chocolate, banks and watches, I now leave, loves."

EPILOGUE

It would be an oversimplification to say that Ripper was destroyed by the Fascism he had fought all his life. To begin with, he was caught up in legal toils he might have been conventional enough to foresee. And Spain, or the Spanish people, have evolved a long way—farther than General Franco has admitted even to himself, one might suspect. But if Spain is no longer a strident Fascist state, it is still filled with Fascists in high position and it was these who, in the end, got their own back at a lifetime enemy, Rudolph Charles von Ripper.

Among his exploits, at the end of World War II, Rip caught Skorzeny, Hitler's pet commando, a bold, brave man. Majorca has, since 1945, been a haven for Nazis afraid to return to democratic Germany and among these was the former chief of Nazi espionage in Catalonia during the war, Skorzeny's friend and an old intimate of Diels of the Gestapo.

I have in my possession the sworn, notarized affidavit of a well-known author, Ripper's friend, which says of this Nazi spy in Catalonia:

"1. That I have personally known 'Schmidt' [a pseudonym] since 1953.

"2. That on Wednesday, November 9, 1960, the following statements were made by Schmidt to me and others.

"a. The late Rudolph von Ripper and his wife were arrested crossing the Spanish frontier at two different points carrying between them a large quantity of heroin said to amount to fifty kilograms.

"b. That the Spanish Government, in order not to embarrass the Rippers had stated that only jewelry had been smuggled. This however was not true because, as is well known, everyone smuggles jewelry across the Spanish frontier.

"c. That subsequently at his home C'an Cueg, Pollensa, Rudolph von Ripper had taken his life by taking poison pills.

"d. That he, Schmidt, had been called in by the police to confirm the cause of death and had identified the pills (presumably those left over) as identical with the suicide pills issued to German intelligence forces during World War II. Furthermore, Schmidt had been able to verify the cause of death through the appearance of the remains of the deceased.

"e. That the Spanish Government in order to avoid em-

barrassment to the widow had given heart failure as the
cause of Ripper's death.

"f. That he, Schmidt, had communicated with several
Spanish officials to try to help quash the case against Mrs.
Ripper, but had been informed that the circumstances of
dope smuggling were so clearly established that nothing
could be done to stop the course of Spanish justice.

"g. That Mrs. Ripper had been taken from the island and
was now believed to be in jail in Madrid awaiting trial."

It was Nazis like Schmidt and others whom I cannot
name for legal reasons of possible libel or slander, and Fascists in the provincial Spanish hierarchy, all of whom had
hated this rebellious, anarchistic Ripper, who made a post-
humous misery for him.

What a strange paradox: Ripper the anti-Fascist chose,
with contemptuous illogic, to build his permanent home in
Fascism's last refuge, Spain. And even when true Fascism
had disappeared from Spain, the remaining Fascists there
were still able to punish him when he could no longer fight,
being dead. Dead Fascism desecrating the system's own
dead enemy; how odd a fate.

A few days after Rip was buried, while tales like
Schmidt's were starting their evil rounds, Avi received a
letter from Germany's honorable new government advising
Ripper he was entitled to a pension of five marks a day for
each day of torture he had suffered in the concentration
camp of Oranienburg so many years ago.

So late; even his corpse had by then been devoured by
intolerance.

Ripper was a Catholic (if, admittedly, not the best).

Nevertheless the local priest would not allow him to be laid to rest within the Catholic cemetery. He was immured inside a thick wall covered with chicken wire where heretics, including two Protestants, are kept: a hideous, grim little plot. The body began to smell in five days. Avi and her friends later bought up the entire plot, whitewashed it and planted it with flowers.

Some time afterward the Pollensa priest, plump as a capon, called on Avi. Drinking a glass of Dubonnet, rubbing his little hands together, he said the housekeeper of a Spanish Fascist had assured him Rip was not a Catholic—although Avi could show his baptismal certificate in Latin, German, Hungarian and English.

Meanwhile Schmidt and his friends spread their dirty tales: that Rip wasn't dead at all (although three hundred persons had seen his corpse in that ugly open coffin) but had escaped to America to avoid a smuggler's trial: that he had committed suicide in disgrace—as proven by the fact that the church would not allow him in hallowed ground; that he was both a heroin peddler and addict. How cruelly and effectively the long and bony arm of Diels, who died of a hunting accident in Katzenelnbogen, extended from grave to grave.

Well, there we are: Ripper; no one dared malign him while he lived. A strange heroic figure, out of his time, who never succumbed to Fascism until both he and it were dead.

I hope I have done justice to the quality of this man; the quality was excellent: a fighter with a stout heart, generous soul and sensitive personality. When his friend Malraux heard of Ripper's death, he told another friend: "The last of the great romantics are dying. Ripper has gone; soon it will be you and me."

Ripper was a misfit. He sought trouble but he never discovered the true meaning of his own life until it was awakened by almost unbearable torture and brutality. At first, as a youngster, he fought for enjoyment, as an escapist mercenary, against the noble and unfortunate Druses. He found his vocation as a fighting man only when he found his great enemy, Fascism, an enemy which in the end trampled upon his defenseless memory. A good man, born and died: perhaps it is just that he, so unorthodox an individual, should lie in a heretic's plot, a misfit also in the death he often faced and spurned.

Now in the Balearics, where the sun rises so suddenly over Minorca to the east, over Port Mahón, from which the chef of the Duc de Richelieu drew the name for his great sauce, mayonnaise, when his patron captured that pleasant harbor; there is Ripper's Majorcan grave, near great wild crags above the briny placid sea, even removed from his garden's scented air, where yet, as my wife so sweetly wrote: "Every leaf is his, every branch, every stone."

If the Resistentialist can live so well and thereby leave behind him such good memories, what does it matter how they posthumously dispose of him, the ones whose very raison d'être he was so active in destroying?

CHAPTER 2

THE BRAVEST COLLABORATOR

"Mine was a terrible decision. No man should be faced with such a choice. . . . I knew when I made my resolve that I would have to pay for it. But it is not fair that a man should have to pay forever."

—MICHEL DUPONT

One day in the spring of 1951, my friend Buck Lanham, a general at Eisenhower's SHAPE headquarters, telephoned me, said he had a problem and asked if I would give him lunch. It has always been a practice of mine to feed generals well, so I took him down to La Boule d'Or on the Place d'Aligre, near the revolutionary bowels of Paris, and I gave him pissaladière, a loup au fenouil, boudin aux pommes en l'air and a poire Hélène, all of which was washed down by Blanc Fumé de Pouilly sur Loire and a bottle of Bouzy, vin nature rouge de Champagne, plus some excellent framboise with the coffee.

Buck Lanham was a regular army officer (since retired) of considerable charm and much wider interests than is usual among American military men. During the war he commanded the regiment which fought through the ter-

rible Hürtgen Forest and made the first deep penetration
of the Siegfried Line. At that time he became a close friend
of Ernest ˙Hemingway. Hemingway first arrived at Buck's
command post as part spectator, part correspondent, part
novelist and also a large part buccaneer who was by no
means above taking an occasional pot shot at the Germans.

Shortly after the two men first met in 1944, they made
a bet as to who would reach a certain Luxembourg village
first, a village then still occupied by the Nazis. Lanham
found a peasant who showed him a side road and there he
was, sipping an apéritif at the local café, when Mr. Ernie,
as the whole regiment came to call him, finally showed up
in his jeep.

An old farmer approached the two of them, sitting there
in the sunlight, proud of themselves and each other. He inquired of each, "Are you the general?" At that time Buck
was still a colonel, but Hemingway told the farmer Lanham
was "the general" while he himself was but a captain. The
farmer regarded Hemingway's graying hair and beard and
asked, "How is it that a man of your years is only a captain?" Mr. Ernie replied, "It is to my eternal shame and
sorrow that I must confess I never learned how to read or
write."

Well, this story got around and Mr. Ernie was very welcome when he rejoined his colleagues among the splintered
trees of the Hürtgenwald. He used to wander among the
troops with two canteens strapped to his belt, one filled
with gin and the other with Noilly Prat, paying no attention
to the noise of battle or the visible results of that noise.

Every now and then he would haul out a battered tin cup and suggest: "Let's have a martini."

Since both Lanham and Hemingway were brave men, and since both of them were given to violating all unnecessary regulations, their companionship was close and marked by mutual esteem. Mr. Ernie showed himself to be a good fighter with all weapons, although, under the Geneva Convention, he was precluded from bearing arms because he was, or pretended to be, a war correspondent. Hemingway used to tell the delighted G.I.'s he was going to have the Geneva Convention tattooed on his ass in reverse so he could read it while looking in a mirror.

A result of this friendship was that Lanham became about 50 per cent of the model for the American colonel who was the hero of Hemingway's novel about Hürtgen and Trieste, *Across the River and into the Trees*. I say 50 per cent because Hemingway himself was always at least 50 per cent the model for all his heroes, whether they were guerrillas, gunmen or merely enormous fish.

All this is a digression but it is the kind of digression inspired by a lunch at La Boule d'Or. Also, as will be seen, it has a reason. Over the framboise, a powerful libation served in carefully iced brandy glasses, a drink enormously more potent than its name might imply, Buck finally came to the point. He explained his problem, the problem that produced this particular lunch. It was simply this. An old friend of his had arrived at SHAPE headquarters two days before and asked for help. He had been in serious trouble and had just emerged from prison. Lanham wished to help

him, but he did not want to embarrass his government or
General Eisenhower.

"I don't see that there is any particular difficulty," I said
brashly. "What was he in for?"

"Collaboration," said Buck, regarding me over the edge
of his glass.

In 1951 the word "collaboration," always a dirty word,
was still especially dirty in France. The country had been
occupied by the Germans for more than four years, and a
considerable minority of Frenchmen at all levels had, in
one way or another, aided or abetted the Nazis. Hundreds
of Frenchmen had actually joined S.S. special forces to
fight under the swastika against the Allies. Thousands of
others had supported a government of pro-Hitler Fascists.
And tens of thousands had refused to help the patriots
fighting for France's honor.

In short, France, that proud nation, had been riddled
with wartime collaborators and even the great ferocity displayed toward those caught, at least initially, could not
erase the stain. Some Frenchmen had merely assumed that
if their army, supposedly Europe's finest, could be so easily
shattered by the Germans, Hitler had automatically won
the war. According to this logic, a quality admired by the
French because so often' they fail to practice it, it was de-
sirable to come to terms as rapidly as possible with the con-
queror and, indeed, to take advantage of France's priority
in defeat. These were the people, the "logical" profiteers,
who made money out of the occupation.

And higher up were the right-wing officials, the sympathizers with the Cagoulards and Croix de Feu, the open and hidden Fascists, the Anglophobes, the savage anti-Communists, who reckoned that France could make a good thing—some thought even a noble thing—out of the ashes of disaster. Of these, Laval was convicted, sought to escape execution by taking poison, had his stomach pumped out and was dragged vomiting and semi-conscious before a firing squad.

On the other hand there were other and finer characters caught up in the vortex of impossible circumstances, brave men who were ignorant, disciplined men who were foolish, decent men who were cowards, and heroes, true heroes, who were faced with impossible choices. All in the end, all who were caught before the waves of passion had subsided, were seen by Blind Justice, to whom revolutionary France once built a temple, as guilty of the sin of treason. There were no brave collaborators.

Immediately after the liberation, the outstanding traitors were rounded up and shot or imprisoned, although thousands of others were able to hide out or lie low long enough to benefit from eventual amnesties. In 1951, a scant six years after V-E Day, "collaborator" was still the foulest label one could fasten on a Frenchman, and the French language is a precise language with a vocabulary rich in foul appellations.

I could, therefore, see Lanham's point. No matter who his friend was, anyone who had collaborated under any circumstances with the Nazis simply could not be helped by an American general at SHAPE, military headquarters of the NATO allies. Were it to become known in France that such a relationship existed between a collaborator and an officer on General Eisenhower's staff, irreparable harm might be done.

I told Buck I was perplexed, to say the least. "Tell me the story," I suggested. We ordered another framboise and this is what he said, all the time observing my reactions through his chilly eyes.

One day last week a Frenchman named Michel Dupont had telephoned Lanham and asked if he could see him. I hasten right now to say that Michel Dupont is not his real name; but it is close enough and it will do.

Dupont had been the jeep driver and self-constituted bodyguard who chauffeured Hemingway from Rambouillet, near Paris, right into the Siegfried Line, and Buck had come to know him well, to like him and respect him; so he gave him an appointment for later in the week.

He had not seen this man, whom both he and Hemingway knew as "Mike," since Germany's collapse. He had heard, as had Hemingway, disquieting rumors for a time, but these had been forgotten and disbelieved—rumors that Dupont was in trouble for having been a collaborator before becoming Mr. Ernie's chauffeur. But both men had filled out glowing testimonials to his courage and loyalty and, hearing nothing further, dropped the matter. They assumed this was part of the frenzied and insane confusion, the bitterness and backbiting, that inflames a country recently freed from enemy occupation and seeking to regain its self-respect. Hemingway returned to his books, fishing and hunting and Lanham moved upward in his officer's career.

Now, said Buck, in anger and frustration, he had heard, first from Hemingway and then from Dupont, six and a half years after the Hürtgen Forest battle, that Michel had been imprisoned on a most ignoble charge. Two days before Dupont's appointment with him, Lanham had received a letter from Hemingway, then living in San Francisco de Paula, Cuba.

Michel had recently informed Mr. Ernie that he had been convicted of giving away to the Gestapo a member of his resistance network. Regretfully Hemingway wrote to Lanham that he felt any man who had done such a contemptible thing, no matter how decent he appeared to be, should have been condemned to death before a firing squad. It was evident that any member of a sensible resistance network was supposed to hold out for twenty-four hours under the most hideous kind of torture so other members of the network could escape to hiding. Clearly this had not been the case with Michel. He had only been imprisoned, which was his good fortune, but he had done the unpardonable thing. Hemingway had brought the matter to Buck's attention because Michel had written saying he intended to call upon the general. Mr. Ernie himself made no recommendation.

Yet in this same letter Hemingway described Dupont as "the bravest man I have ever known." Indeed, Hemingway said, he had found Michel so entirely fearless that he sometimes wondered whether he was trying to get himself killed.

He decided this was not the case because Dupont was "cheerful brave." And Hemingway concluded a "cheerful brave" man is not deliberately seeking suicide. He is merely filled with courage.

Michel had always explained to Hemingway that he particularly hated the Germans because they had mistreated his Jewish wife. Dupont himself was not Jewish. As far as Hemingway was concerned, this seemed a satisfactory explanation and an eminently reasonable one, above all coming from a Frenchman. Hemingway, like anyone who saw World War I and lived in Paris afterward, entertained vast respect and admiration for the French.

Buck had seen Dupont at a rendezvous arranged away from SHAPE. And Dupont confirmed what Hemingway had written in his letter—that he had betrayed a member of his resistance group before becoming Mr. Ernie's driver and later had been sent to prison for it.

General Lanham was astounded by his old friend's appearance. Michel's face had that peculiar, dead, fish-belly pallor that comes from being shut up in a cell. His gaze was no longer clear or steady. He was thin, nervous, twitchy. He needed help; and he said he needed help. He added, "I have no friends."

"I was horrified," Buck told me, "horrified and embarrassed. But I want to help the poor bastard. No matter what crime he committed, I know he has quality. There is something terrible behind this. Yet I can't go further in the matter. All we need at SHAPE is to have word get around France that an American general is aiding a convicted collaborator. I can't do that to Ike. And I won't. That's where I need your help."

"How?" I asked.

"I want you to see this guy. Listen to his story. Try to think of something for him. Anything. He's broke. He has no friends. He has no family. He no longer knows anyone. Anyone who knew him before automatically turns his back when they meet. And every time he tries to get a job, the union finds out from his employment card that he's been in the coop as a 'collabo.' Then he's fired.

"Now what can I do? All I can say is this. When I knew him and as I knew him, he was a fine fellow. Will you help? Will you at least help to the degree of finding out what lies behind all this?"

I agreed.

That night, it so happened, I had dinner with, among others, Hervé Tillion, a very excellent Frenchman, who had until recently been head of the Sûreté, the equivalent of our own F.B.I. Tillion, a quiet intellectual, possessed a splendid wartime resistance record. I told him the story of Michel Dupont as I had heard it.

Dupont, I told him, had fought well in the French Army until France's defeat. After being demobilized he had been connected with a resistance network and had somehow been induced to turn over one of his comrades to the Nazis. Nevertheless, when Hemingway and Lanham had come to know him later, and to know him well, they were immensely impressed with his courage and his patriotism.

As soon as the word "collaborator" intruded into the

conversation, Tillion grew vastly suspicious. He was not impressed by my account of Michel's record of bravery, despite the testimony of both Hemingway and Lanham. Indeed, he was more impressed by Hemingway's wisdom in disassociating himself from Michel's fate and cautioning Lanham than by the general's judgment in agreeing to see Dupont at all.

"You say he was arrested twice by the Gestapo," said Tillion. "I cannot believe he had any real resistance value after the first arrest. I can assure you on this point; and I can assure you on the basis of my own experience. I headed one extensive resistance network and I know whereof I speak.

"Even the Gestapo, despite its rigid training methods, never trusted any of its agents after they had been in Russian hands more than twenty-four hours. The Gestapo assumed it was possible to break a man's spirit and his loyalty so completely and effectively within that period of time that, if he escaped later, there was too great a risk he had become a double agent or in some other way was subject to Soviet blackmail. In fact, the Germans considered a man very dubious if the Russians had held him more than three hours.

"Clearly this Dupont you talk of, after his first arrest, was probably a plant. I don't care what he did afterward, how agreeable he was, how courageously he behaved, how sad his tale may be, how reasonable his case may sound. There is something strange about this story. That man is lucky he wasn't shot."

This may sound hard and cruel but I can assure you

Tillion is neither hard nor cruel. You must remember the atmosphere that still prevailed six years after a terrible war in which thousands of Frenchmen, quite apart from the fighting forces, lost their lives to Nazi torturers.

Our conversation occurred at a party given by a French diplomat. In his apartment overlooking the Gothic spires of St. Germain des Prés, our host had assembled several French Cabinet ministers, diplomatists, officers and intellectuals. I was therefore astounded when Tillion, the former security chief, scanned this distinguished gathering and said, "Apropos of the man about whom you were talking, you can never trust anyone. In my business you learn this simple fact. You cannot even trust people who have never been imprisoned by the Nazis or the Communists. I will tell you exactly what I mean. There is one man here at this party who has not been a prisoner of either; yet I can assure you we suspect he is a Soviet agent."

This was startling. I looked about. There were perhaps eighteen women and eighteen men, the *haut monde* of France, not one of them lacking in either renown or reputation.

"What can you mean?" I inquired.

Tillion replied, "Have you the vaguest idea of how an unwilling agent is manufactured? How a good patriot can be turned into a traitor?"

I answered in the negative.

"Let me give you an example," he continued. "There is a certain operation called prefrontal lobotomy." He described this in great detail. The surgery was brutally simple. An icepick or some similar instrument was inserted in the tear ducts just above the victim's eye and driven upward into the brain. The result was a definite alteration in the victim's personality. He was then infinitely more subject to direction along new psychological lines, in fact subject to external dictation without himself being aware of this. He became a sort of zombie, soulless but alive. Yet no one, not even his own family, could measure the degree of change.

This surgical treatment had, indeed, been known for many years and was once not infrequently applied to otherwise incurable psychiatric cases. But it was made familiar as a weapon of war, and then only rarely, by twentieth-century dictatorships. There was virtually no way of telling whether such an operation had been performed on a person who had fallen into enemy hands.

For a day or two he had what seemed to be two ordinary black eyes. Nevertheless, unless there were available electro-encephalographic charts of impulses in the subject's brain, recorded previously and when he was quite normal, charts that could be compared with similar graphs made after a secret prefrontal lobotomy, it was impossible to be sure of such maltreatment. There was no permanent scar. And the subject himself was wholly unaware of what had been done to him. Apparently the only absolute confirmation of such devilish usages came after the war when all this was done to an Englishman picked up in Poland and later released. Fortunately, there existed an earlier electroencephalogram of the poor man's brain.

After our grim discussion, during which my eye continually roved over the chattering guests in search of the suspected agent, Tillion promised as a special favor that he would look up Dupont's record. Although he had recently left the Sûreté, he would arrange to have the files sent on to me. But, as we parted, he admonished, "I remain very skeptical. I doubt your wisdom in taking an interest in this case."

That summer found me traveling a great deal, far from France. I nevertheless continued to pursue the subject. Tillion sent me the official records on Michel Dupont. Dupont himself came to see me several times and I tried unsuccessfuly to help him find employment, first in France and then in Switzerland. And I entered into a lengthy correspondence about him with Hemingway.

Not long after my initial conversations with Lanham and Tillion I wrote to Hemingway as follows.

"Recently I lunched with Buck and he told me, in broad outline, the story of Michel Dupont from the days he first knew him until the present, including the sad episode of his conviction for collaboration. I have since seen Dupont several times and have gotten from him his own account of his personal history.

"I want to write a story about Dupont in an effort to show, through his own individual case, the huge problem that still exists in Europe as a result of the psychological scars of war which have not been eradicated. Also I want to try and help Michel get some sort of a job so that he can try and make a new life for himself.

"I would deeply appreciate it if you could send me a brief account of Michel's behavior as a fighting man while he was with you. Furthermore, could you give me your own opinion concerning the psychological reasons for his courage as related to his prior tragedy and your thoughts concerning his behavior in the dual role of a member of the resistance and then a collaborator?"

From Finca Vigia, Hemingway's Cuban home, the author replied with great frankness, the start of a lengthy correspondence I was to have with him on the subject of Michel Dupont. Unfortunately, some time before his death Ernest, or Papa, as he liked to be called, wrote a special testament in his own hand categorically forbidding publication of his letters. This is a pity, for all the warmth and vigor of his personality emerges in them. And no one, in recollection or in paraphrase, can recapture the uninhibited originality of his style.

Hemingway admitted it was not easy for him to write about Dupont because their two destinies had been so closely intertwined during a savage period of war. They were always together and Hemingway felt embarrassed about praising Michel's audacity. By inference, it seemed to him, this might almost look like self-praise since he was all too often by Dupont's side. And, prior to the Battle of the Bulge, Ernest had been investigated—and cleared—of charges that he was serving as more than an unarmed war correspondent but had, on occasion, commanded irregular troops and fought with them against the Nazis. I venture to suspect there was something in the allegations. Hemingway was both fearless and unrestrained.

Ernest reminded me that Michel had been with him all the way from Rambouillet, near Paris, to the Siegfried Line in the Rhineland, sometimes guarding the famous author, sometimes fighting, sometimes scouting, sometimes taking part in special commando raids. He showed great capacity as a soldier, often volunteering for actions exceeding his normal duties, and establishing himself as a particular hero in the grim Schnee-Eifel.

Hemingway recalled that Dupont had driven his jeep during the Hürtgen Forest battle, also acting as a bodyguard and doing some extracurricular shooting on his own. Michel, although French, had been enrolled as a kind of special servitor of Hemingway in those informal days when thousands of Frenchmen were given false documents, American uniforms and a chance to kill Germans. Michel, technically speaking, served with the 4th U.S. Infantry Division. But he took his orders directly from Hemingway. He wore a uniform stripped from the back of a dead G.I. who had been ambushed with an armored cavalry unit not far from Rambouillet.

Michel's past was then not known to Hemingway. At that time men were taken on trust if they seemed willing. There was little formal screening of French volunteers. Everyone was too preoccupied with the constant probes of German tanks and motorized troops seeking to frustrate the steady advance and allow time for the main retreat.

Michel just showed up one day driving a German lorry and expressing eagerness to fight. Hemingway recognized him as a soldier who knew his trade. He was filled with ardor and determination, but he did not *seem* to be courting death foolishly. He wanted to kill, but not to be killed himself in some silly way. He ignored his own safety when necessary, but only then. Hemingway didn't bother to interrogate him. He knew merely that Dupont's wife was

Jewish and that she had suffered something dreadful during the occupation; that was all.

Hemingway had been on a special assignment from *Collier's* magazine, sending them one piece a month and, as he modestly remembered, trying to be helpful on the side. His talents and experience in warfare were widely recognized and he was regarded as somewhat of an expert on guerrilla tactics. Sometimes he carefully shucked off his correspondent's insignia and left his press credentials behind when he thought his methods of trying to be "helpful on the side" might conceivably embarrass the position of other newspapermen. You can imagine what this is meant to imply. And he found Michel helpful in such schemes.

It never occurred to him that Dupont was trying to ease his conscience of some heavy burden. But, when he wrote me about this period, Hemingway pointed out that if this indeed had been the case, there were others. Hadn't the son of a renowned French general been accused of collaboration? And didn't the father fight with especial ardor when he learned that dismal news?

Hemingway was distressed by the problem of Michel. He begged me not to mention his real name, should I write anything about him, and to enlist Buck Lanham's aid in trying to rebuild him as a confident citizen of victorious France.

During the rest of the summer, I travelled a good deal. But, in addition to maintaining contact with the pathetic Dupont, whom I tried to get a job in Switzerland where he might start life anonymously and afresh, I continued my correspondence with Hemingway. He sent me a long and moving letter on August 10, 1951, again from Finca Vigia. This was remarkable not only for its concern with Michel's fate but also for the fact he took pains to express such concern when he, too, was having troubles.

His mother had died. His father-in-law was in the hospital with an incurable illness. And he was working desperately hard on a new book, pouring out thousands of words each day, editing them, rewriting them, throwing them away and starting again. I once talked to Ernest about this business of writing. He admitted he found it tedious, difficult work, standing up each morning before a specially-constructed high desk, forcing himself to stay there, scribbling, patting his typewriter, even if nothing came at all or if what finally emerged failed the test of his self-critical eye. He had written, re-written and re-rewritten 14,857 words during an arduous ten days.

Ernest was concerned lest Michel's crime should again be advertised. He was also worried lest I should write something about it, even giving him a pseudonym, that might make Hemingway seem too pretentious or vainglorious, simply because he had been in all the same hellish scrapes with Dupont from Rambouillet through the Hürtgen and the Siegfried Line. Indeed, Hemingway had a strange sensitivity on this subject. He wrote about heroes and it is patently obvious that each of these characters was at least in part himself. Yet he had a morbid self-consciousness about making himself out to be a hero in fact. He explained that once Malcolm Cowley had been assigned by *Life* to write an article about him but Hemingway found it quite impossible to answer any questions concerning his own role on the battlefields he knew. It nauseated him, he said.

He was also anxious lest any delving into Michel's previous history might expose further ugliness. For he knew Dupont only as an exceptionally valorous, devoted friend who had had bad luck. It made him almost sick to think that things lay behind this picture, things that might disappoint or hurt those friends of Michel who knew him as a gallant hero. He even wondered if he, Hemingway, might not be well advised himself to write the story some day. What a pity he never had a chance to do so.

I replied, saying: "Michel cannot forget the past or be forgotten, tragic as this may sound. He has found it impossible to get work in France. I am now trying to help him get a job in Geneva. Incidentally, he wrote me nine days ago and said he has written to you more than once but had not received any reply."

Hemingway answered that he hadn't written Dupont for the simple reason that he didn't know quite what to say. He had not seen the dossier Tillion sent me and he was unable to imagine all the circumstances. Had Michel been forced by unbearable tortures to break down and talk? If so, that could be understood and humanly forgiven. Had he feared so for the safety of his family that he had collapsed and put the finger on a friend? Or had it been fear? Or ambition? Or some kind of bribe? This thing was beginning to turn uncomfortably in Ernest's mind.

Then too, he could not but remember, wars and revolutions can bring out the full malevolence of men. There were false denunciations just as there were traitors who had never been denounced. And vicious people took vengeance for petty feuds by spreading lies and gossip. Was it possible Dupont had been caught up in that kind of evil network? After all, he had never been an angel, nor were the people with whom he had once associated. Hemingway wondered if there had not been a kind of emotional Terror after the war, like the Terror that devoured so many decent Frenchmen in the Revolution.

All he knew, in his own heart, was that Michel was a fine man when they were together and this was a memory he treasured. Michel, on his own account, had sought out far more dangerous corners of the battlefield than any to which Ernest might have sent him. Moreover he went to these ghastly hellholes with a light heart, much skill and no apparent thought of suicide. If he was devil-may-care, he was nevertheless as proficient as any soldier may be on the edge of death. It was the kind of bravery Hemingway felt he could trust, in terms of the inner truth of a man's character. And Hemingway knew much of bravery.

I remember years later discussing this subject of courage with Ernest over a bottle of wine in his favorite Paris bistro. In a way he seemed obsessed by it, perhaps because it was such an incalculable and unpredictable—aye human —aspect. Some men could be heroes under certain circumstances and ineffable cowards under others. And yet they were one and the same. He talked at length and reached no conclusions except, tossing off a final glass, the absurd remark that all brave men had long noses. Hemingway didn't and he was very brave.

Once he wrote that he thought he had judged Dupont's

character with acuity (not the kind of word Ernest would have used but then I can't, alas, quote his priceless letters.) He found during his experience of war that those excellent soldiers, the irregulars, had always to be *débrouillard*, and that the true irregular, in an irregular situation, had to be able to scramble in and out of things, including death, with complete insouciance. This led him to reflect on what had happened to these *débrouillards* when peace again embraced them. He suspected, when considering the fate of Michel Dupont, that many of the best had suffered worst in civil life.

He came to ponder more and more on this tawdry possibility and Michel's own tale began to draw up other similar sad stories from the recesses of his mind, stories he would have preferred to forget. I have a disquieting feeling that Hemingway, who was just then perhaps beginning his own time of troubles, a time that ended a decade later with his unconquerable illness and infinitely tragic death, was thrown off balance by the sordid implications of the Dupont incident and the gates of horror and injustice that it opened.

Ernest could never rid himself of the conviction that Michel was cheerful brave, as he would put it, and therefore sane, balanced and of essentially good conscience. I cannot quarrel with this logic which is eminently sensible. But I suppose it all goes to show how wrong an artist may be when, by the necessary feat of imagination, he injects himself into another's soul. I am only glad for the sake of both men that Hemingway and Dupont never met again after Michel left prison. He didn't look either cheerful or brave.

The Bravest Collaborator

Hemingway certainly gave the impression of carefree cheer. When things were going badly, he wrote, with plain philosophy, that his wife's father seemed a good deal better but this was only temporary, for he was doomed; and what, he inquired, was not temporary after all? He was planning to come to Paris and hoped to swipe the card of a famous movie actress, a friend of his, so as to send it in to General Lanham's office at SHAPE with a scribbled and insulting message. But he had looked around and discovered he had no cards. So maybe it might be better just to kidnap Buck, hold him for ransom, and send a fanciful communique to the tabloid press, hoping for a jovial scandal. Ah, that was a nice man, as well as a talented one!

I decided that Ernest should be told, for his own sake if for no other reason, just what the official police record on Michel Dupont was. He knew him so well and, during that brutal but glorious period of an ending war, he was so intimately entangled with this pathetic if also noble little man, that he had a right if not an obligation to all the facts as coldly listed in what an emotionless state calls history. So I wrote:

"For your own confidential information I am enclosing copies of the Sureté reports on Michel and a fellow named Blanc, the French Gestapo agent who turned him in and gave him the horrible choice between fingering a resistance colleague, head of a small network, or seeing his family go to perdition.

"I am not supposed to have these reports, so I would be grateful if you would destroy them after you have read them. As you will see, Michel does not appear to be a complete Chevalier Bayard, but, on the other hand, I have reason to believe that the reports are neither 100% accurate, nor sufficiently extensive. They were naturally made during the immediate period of post-war hysteria."

At this point I must insert in this curious and sad correspondence a portion of a letter written to me at my request by General Lanham. If nothing else, it will confirm from another brave man the record of Dupont's courage. Buck wrote:

"Of course, you have heard a good deal about the battle of Hürtgen Forest. It is reputed to be the bloodiest battle in which American troops were engaged during World War II. Ernie and Michel were with us throughout our deadly 18 days and 18 nights in this gloomy forest of endless terror and sudden death. Neither one had to be there. During this agonizing and heartbreaking period, Michel Dupont fought with conspicuous gallantry—this, I know of my own knowledge, because I personally saw him engaged on several occasions. He volunteered for hazardous patrols. He assisted with the wounded, and he was back and forth over deadly trails in that forest day in and day out.

"One morning about six days after the battle adjourned, I was returning from a first-hand look at our forward positions when I heard a hell of a fight back of me: i.e., in my Command Post area. I hot-footed it back there and found that the Command Post proper had been jumped at close range by a number of Krauts who had hidden within a hundred yards or so of this critical installation for at least two days.

"It was a brisk little affair while it went on. Clerks, messengers, drivers, everyone got mixed up in the scrap. When I arrived on the scene, Michel was in the forefront of the fighting and it was fighting at pretty damned close range, often at grenade range. My Headquarters Commandant had gathered up a handful of miscellaneous people at the headquarters when the first shot hit and had torn into the Krauts.

"He had kept on going, under the assumption that all the people were behind him. They weren't. The result was the Krauts mowed him down. Michel came on the scene just at this time. No one was sure whether the Captain was alive or dead. He was well liked and it was obvious that if someone didn't get to him and bring him back he would die. The fighting was still hot, but the Krauts were giving a little ground. Michel never asked anyone anything but simply took off on his own and made a beeline for the Captain. No one expected him to get there alive, but miraculously enough he did. The Captain was dead. Michel survived his trip and fought like a dragon until the attack was beaten off and the Krauts harassed and pursued through the woods. I saw part of this action personally and many of my people saw all of it. All testified to Michel's gallantry.

"Throughout the ordeal of Hürtgen, there was scarcely a day that went by that he didn't lay his life on the line in one way or another. All of my people who saw him were deeply impressed with him. It is my opinion that he individually instilled more belief in my people concerning the fighting qualities of the Frenchman than any other person or, for that matter, group of people. He was a living affirmation of the French will to fight and a constant testimonial to the Frenchman's deadliness in a fight, given any sort of chance at all.

"Michel was with us in September of 1944 when we stormed and breached the Siegfried in the Prüm area. Here again he was in and out of the fight all the time. He would ask Ernest for permission to go up to the front for a while. He hated the Germans with a living passion. He took more pleasure and derived more satisfaction from their steady string of defeats at our hands than any man I ever saw.

"Ernie is completely correct when he says that Michel went with him on his wild dash from Paris up to my regiment during the height of the Bulge. He did, indeed. And here, again, he was all over the front, out on patrols, mixing up in dangerous situations, etc., etc.—all on a voluntary basis. To the best of my knowledge, no one ever asked him to volunteer for anything or ever urged him to do anything. All that he did during the long period of time that he and Ernie were with my regiment was done out of his own sense of the fitness of things and his desire to fight in our common cause. From beginning to end his conduct was honorable and gallant. I never heard one complaint concerning him. And my people were quick to complain if they didn't like anything.

"When I first learned from Ernie that Michel had been accused of collaboration, I was both incredulous and indignant, so was Ernie. It seemed impossible. It seemed to be nothing more than one of the wild denunciations that jealous people often leveled against their neighbors in the confused days following the German capitulation. In fact, I felt so strongly on the subject and was so impressed with

Michel's conduct during the time he and Ernest were with my regiment that I wrote a testimonial of some length and sent it to Michel for such use as he wished to make of it. I know that Ernie did the same thing. I was confident that the whole affair was a mistake and that Michel would never be brought to trial. Neither Ernie nor I heard anything more of it and we simply assumed that he had again found his place in the civilian community and was busy re-establishing himself.

"I learned his story in May, 1951, and a shocking and heart-breaking story it was. To my mind, this obscure Frenchman—the true little man of Europe—epitomizes the fearful travail of the age in which we live. Certainly now more than ever all men would do well to remember the essential truth of the old French proverb: 'To understand all is to forgive all.' "

My own effort to understand Michel Dupont was far from easy. From the first time he called upon me in my office I found him shy, furtive and mistrustful, like a dog too often kicked. His personality gave no hint of the fire that must have glowed within him during the days when he made an exceptional name for audacity as a soldier even among audacious men. After our initial talk on a June morning in 1951, I jotted down the following brief impression:

"Michel Dupont is a neatly dressed and rather average-looking Frenchman of 39. Only his eyes, sad and somewhat watery, mirror his torment. His face is yellow like a cellar-grown mushroom. He clearly has no shred of inner confidence. And when you look at him, he looks away."

Michel admitted, haltingly, that he had just been released from the prison of Igrec (another name I have disguised), where he had spent the years since victory. He was sent there because he betrayed his good friend Jacques to the Gestapo. Jacques was in a resistance network with Dupont, who turned him in for a simple human reason: to save the lives of his own wife and baby.

Now, six years after the war, Michel was still a "collaborator," one of the thousands upon thousands in Europe who had survived the swift, cruel, passionate justice meted out to traitors. He remained condemned to the category of "ineligible"—those who were again free but could not vote, had neither legal nor civil rights, were jobless because employers feared to hire them and friendless because their former companions were ashamed to associate with them.

Michel told me, squeezing out every word: "Mine was a terrible decision. No man should be faced with such a choice. And yet, had I to do it over again, I would have to take the same horrible road. I knew when I made my resolve that I would have to pay for it. But it is not fair that a man should have to pay forever."

The Serbian hero Drazha Mihailovitch perhaps best expressed the conditions which overwhelmed Michel. In July, 1946, when the Chetnik leader made a final statement to the Communist court which sentenced him to death for collaboration and crimes against the state, he sadly said: "Fate was merciless to me when it threw me into this maelstrom. I wanted much, I started much. But the whirlwind, the whirlwind of the world, carried me and my work away."

Michel Dupont had nothing in common with Mihailo-vitch. And his work was but the humdrum work of existence and survival, small affairs, small loves, and tragedies ignored by the world. But he was engulfed by the same whirlwind which swept Europe and which left in its wake bitter passions, warped personalities and souls harboring misery and confusion.

Dupont was born in Senlis on August 1, 1911, and married twenty-six years later to a girl of the Jewish faith. He had one daughter, born in February, 1940, just before France was overwhelmed.

Before the German attack, Michel was a film cutter living in Garches, near Paris. He was called up in September, 1939, as an infantry private in the 103rd Regiment of the 3rd Division and sent to the front at Warndt in Germany, just southeast of the Maginot Line. In May, 1940, he volunteered into a commando unit at Sedan and, from all accounts, fought well when the Phony War ended in the West. He was one of nine survivors (seven of them wounded) to reach Villers-Cotterets as the beaten French army withdrew southward. It was he who brought back with him his wounded lieutenant.

When Pétain surrendered, Dupont was in Guéret, near Limoges. He was demobilized and slipped across the line into the occupied portion of the country to join his family, which had moved to a place near Alençon, in Normandy. There he prepared to live the trying existence of the conquered. He borrowed money and purchased a poultry incubator to raise chickens. However, six months later fire destroyed everything just as the first birds were ready to be sold. He decided to return to Paris with his wife to seek a job in the one business he knew, films.

Shortly after his return he met some friends who had already formed a small resistance group. They asked him to join. But Dupont said no. He felt it was too risky because of his wife's religion; he dared not expose her. His friends pressed him. At least, they said, he could arrange for food parcels to be sent through his Normandy connections to their clandestine members, barred from their ration cards.

This he agreed to do. A little later he was asked: Couldn't he help distribute some anti-German tracts? Yes. For that he was also willing. And through his links with the film world and photography, could he not aid in providing false identity papers? He agreed. *De facto*, although he never formalized his allegiance, Dupont, a patriotic man, found himself, against his inclinations, part of a resistance network. The movement was nonpolitical in a party sense. It included many former officers. It was not Communist. Michel himself had entertained right-wing opinions and once belonged to the reactionary, De La Rocque, Croix de Feu.

The first time Dupont was arrested was in February, 1943. Some of the tracts he had been distributing were found by the Gestapo and traced back to him. At seven o'clock one morning two German agents in civilian clothes came to his small apartment. After searching it, they found some leaflets hidden under the staircase carpet outside his front door. They took him to Gestapo headquarters in France's Ministry of the Interior on the Rue des Saussaies in Paris.

Already this office, widely known by the whispered identification "Rue des Saussaies," had a horrifying reputation. It was here that the Nazis had gathered their Gestapo and their Sicherheitsdienst and all the other ghastly, clangorous apparatus of oppression. People who lived in the neighborhood could not sleep at night; the screaming kept them awake.

For the first day, Dupont was alone in a cell. The second day he was moved to a cellar room with about twenty other suspects. He was questioned thoroughly but denied knowing anything about the tracts found beneath the carpet outside his flat. Then he was sent to the prison of Igrec, where he spent six months in solitary confinement.

He was not allowed to write to anyone. The books he received were few. He spent most of his time ruminating and unsuccessfully seeking to strike up conversations with the Alsatian trusty who brought him food twice daily. Then one day a German came into his cell, told him to put his few belongings together, made him sign the prison book and announced that he was free.

Michel returned to Paris, collected his family from a refuge in Normandy and resumed his normal occupation—life. A friend of his named Jacques, also working in the cinema business, was at that time active in the resistance group with which Dupont had previously been associated. Dupont had helped Jacques when he was hiding from the Germans by sending him food and false papers. Now Jacques asked him to resume his underground work and he did—until he was arrested a second time in November, 1943. This is Michel's account of that event:

"I had some friends from my resistance group who used to meet every Friday around 6 P.M. in a little bar near the Place Vendôme. One day in November I went early— maybe around five. I ordered a drink and while I was waiting a man named Blanc came in, accompanied by a woman whom he presented to me as his secretary and who he said was English. Maybe that was queer but I suppose it didn't particularly strike me to find an Englishwoman in occupied Paris. I'm not very clever, you know.

"I knew this man Blanc as leftish, a fellow from the C.G.T. [labor confederation] and a Free Mason. He also had been in films so I knew something about him. He was even a 'venerable' among the Masons. I assumed from all this that he was still against the Germans. He said he was organizing a resistance group and he asked me if I wouldn't help.

"I said I would do what I could. I told him I knew some other resistance men and he said he would like to meet them. I said I would give them his telephone number and then it was up to them. I also made the mistake of telling him I had hidden away some arms in Normandy: four or five rifles, an automatic and some grenades. They were left with my mother and wife by retreating French units in 1940 so I covered them with fat and buried them in the ground.

"On the very next day I was arrested again. And again it was two men in civilian clothes, a little fat one and a thin one, both from the Gestapo. We had a two-room apartment and the cleaning woman used to come at seven o'clock in the morning. I was in bed with my wife when

I heard the bell ring, so I jumped out thinking it was the woman, opened the door quickly and jumped back in the bed. I turned around and saw the two men. They said they were German police. They ordered me into the other room and left my wife in bed. One man questioned me and the other questioned her. They asked about tracts and false documents and the arms I had told Blanc about. We said nothing and they ordered me to come with them. I knew this was really serious.

"While I was getting ready one of the Germans, the fat one, saw a picture of the Pope I had on one wall and he asked: 'Isn't that a Jew?' Then he turned to my wife and said: 'You are a Jew too.' 'Yes,' she replied. He said: 'That is too bad for you.' I asked them if they were going to arrest my wife and this German said: 'I am an officer and they are making me do things I do not like. But I am human.'

"They took me once again to the Rue des Saussaies. On the first day they just asked me questions. On the second day they started beating me. There were big cellars there with little closets where they used to lock you up alone. You could just sit and think.

"The two men who had arrested me were the ones who did the questioning. The first day the little fat fellow who had been decent about my wife seemed sort of kind. He asked if I wasn't hungry. Then he bought me two apples and some cigarettes.

"Oddly enough, it was the same little fat fellow who started to beat me. He asked me again about the weapons and then he punched me suddenly so that I fell down. Then they both beat me. Then they made me take my

111

shoes off and forced me to kneel on the rim of a bicycle wheel without any spokes. The edge hurt my knees.

"They beat my feet with wooden rulers and, when I moved, the rim of the wheel would slip up and bang me in the face. Then they began to burn my legs with lit cigars. I still have the scars. Finally, when I lost consciousness they threw water on me and took me to a bathroom where they tied my arms and held my head under the water.

"I didn't talk. I didn't tell them anything.

"For days they kept taking me back and forth between the Rue des Saussaies and the Igrec prison and beating me. Finally, they made me sign a paper stating I had nothing to do with the resistance. I didn't mind doing that under those conditions. Then they left me alone in a room with the door open. I thought they wanted to see if I was going to try to escape. But someone came into the room. It was Blanc.

"Blanc didn't seem to be in the least bit embarrassed. He was just cynical. When he saw my bruises he said, 'My friend, this is war. We have to build a new Europe.' "

It was only long afterward that Dupont learned that this traitor and Gestapo agent, Blanc, had been personally responsible for the arrest, during the war, of 280 French patriots who were sent to Germany and disappeared. Then he knew but this: that Blanc had held an office in the cinematic union of the C.G.T.; that he had been fired and replaced by Jacques and that clearly Blanc was now a Nazi stooge.

Blanc told Michel that if he signed a pledge not to work against the German Army and the collaborationist Doriot party he would be freed. Michel agreed. Then Blanc said, and here one must again use Dupont's words:

" 'I have one other little thing to ask you. You know Jacques. I know you meet him from time to time. You must help me find him so I can arrest him.'

" 'But, Blanc,' I replied, 'you are asking something I can't do. I have promised many things, but this I cannot do.' Then Blanc said: 'Right now there is a car parked in front of your house with two men sitting in it waiting for my instructions to take your Jewish wife and child away. I know you have no telephone in your apartment but there is one in the café below. Now shall I call them and tell them to arrest your wife and baby? You know what that means for Jews. Or will you arrange a rendezvous with Jacques?'

"I did not break from the torture or the beating. But I thought of my wife and baby. . . .

"They took me to Igrec and then back to the Rue des Saussaies and I was fed and allowed to wash. They kept me until Friday afternoon and then they put me in a car with two German agents. Poor Jacques didn't know I had been arrested again. My wife didn't know where to reach him to advise him.

"So they sat me at the back of a café at a table and they stayed in a corner near the door. And Jacques came in and walked right up to me. And they arrested him. He was my friend. He never came back."

Now this is the dreadful substance of Michel Dupont's crime. There is, of course, but one blind patriotic course to take: to consign your family to the Nazi gas chambers rather than betray the cause of your own ravaged country. But how many men are there who would do this?

Before they crushed him utterly, stole his dignity, this weak, insignificant little man who, to his own surprise, turned out to be so fine upon the battlefield, they dressed him in a nice suit and drove him in a curtained Mercedes car past the entrance to his apartment house. There he saw a Gestapo auto waiting, with four uniformed men inside, waiting for his wife and baby in case he should change his mind. For Michel it was Jacques (with a chance, he rationalized, to live) or his own wife and baby, doomed irrevocably.

It is hard, after all these years, to imagine the agonies of Dupont. Now again we are at peace, all of us who managed to survive, except for people like Michel, whose souls were eviscerated.

Dupont is not a gifted talker but a slow stutterer with a limited vocabulary and no self-confidence. Even the customary Gallic gesture has been driven from his listless hands: a poor, humiliated creature, with skin the color of a lemon floating in the Seine, and all the horrible diseases of confinement: dandruff, watery eyes, and that dreary halitosis that comes of insufficient diet.

And yet you must imagine through his pauciloquent recollections that cold November morning, the unheated tiny apartment, the deadly dull wearing struggle for existence, the sheer hopelessness of hope, the nothingness of a lightless city used to light; a wife, a baby, a few friends, and a gray pervading fear; a conviction that he, Michel Dupont, who sought to escape his fate through rural chicken farming, was born unlucky and was destined to remain so.

Unlike other animals, some of which can communicate both thought and feeling by the wiggling of toes, the waggling of tails, the rubbing of leg joints, the bristling of hair, the extension of antennae and the expression of deep, internal rumbles, mankind has come essentially to rely on speech, on the articulation of precise words to convey imprecise thoughts and memories. And therefore an unlettered man like Dupont is at a disadvantage. He can feel and suffer; and yet he cannot explain to others what this means. A dumb look creeps into his inflamed eyes, an intellectual muteness clutches his voice.

How are we to comprehend cruel remembrances we cannot share? The sound of gagging and of moaning that reverberates so dully from cell to cell in a brutal Gestapo beehive; the smell of vomit, of sweat, of blood, of urine, of stale air and of fear; the blank look on the jailer's face and the merry look upon the torturer's; the keen uncertainty of what is coming next; and the ignorance, that strange untested ignorance, of what one's own soul can bear before it yields.

I talked about these things interminably with Michel, drawn by increasing fascination into the vortex of an occupation and its agonies. But he could tell me little. To tell, to really tell, requires artistry, a Goya or a Dostoievsky, not a plain Dupont. He could recall but technical details, like a garage mechanic explaining how to drain a carburetor. Yet, when it came to telling how a personality is drained, as his was drained, the man was helpless.

To be sure, I sought to open windows in his mind. One

day I said: "Tell me, Mike [as he liked to be called—this nostalgia for the old days with the 22nd U.S. Infantry], how do you make false papers for the underground?"

A faint hint of smile, a momentary confidence, and then: "That is quite easy. The main thing is to find a man or woman of about the same age as the person for whom the papers are required. I'd go to the Mairie and ask for a certificate of birth. You could doctor this, forge it, and with that certificate it wasn't hard to get a residence card. And I would send it to the Prefecture of Police with two photographs to be signed. We had a woman in the Mairie. She was part of our little outfit. Ah yes, that was easy."

Another time I asked him: "Were you allowed to read or write in Igrec Prison?"

He replied: "No, I couldn't write. And I wasn't allowed to ask for anything. The only person I saw was that Alsatian, the man I associate with soup. He never spoke. He too was frightened."

"And what other food did they give you?"

"In the morning coffee. But it wasn't coffee; just dirty water. At 11 A.M. there was that soup. At 4 we got some bread and grease. Not butter, grease. Sometimes a plate of vegetables."

"Could you read?"

"Occasionally they'd give you a book, one they chose. Most of the time there was nothing. Just sit and think."

One day I fortified Michel with a drink. Even before the police file arrived I had detected in him a certain fondness for this consolation. "Mike," I asked, as he emptied the glass, "how about torture? Was it that in the end that maybe helped to break you?"

"It was hard," he said. "They always started by beating me with that wooden ruler on the feet as I kneeled on the bicycle wheel. After that, they'd burn my legs with cigars. Especially when they were trying to find out about the arms I'd hidden, the arms I mentioned to Blanc. If those arms had belonged to somebody else, maybe I would have confessed. That I admit. But I knew that to confess I had those arms was the same as committing suicide.

"Usually, after perhaps three quarters of an hour, I would become unconscious. They'd carry me to a bathroom and throw water on me. They'd put me in the bathtub and fill it up with water. They'd tie my hands behind my back and push my head under until I couldn't breathe. By then I wouldn't exactly know what was happening. Other prisoners told me they used electric wires to give shocks. But I don't think they did that to me. I really couldn't tell."

One afternoon I asked Michel if there was any special reason why Blanc might have had it in for Jacques. Michel said: "That fellow Blanc was once first secretary of our union, until he got fired. He was replaced by Jacques. This made him furious. Maybe he and Jacques quarreled openly. I don't know. At any rate Blanc said to me: 'You know Jacques. You see him sometimes. Give me a chance to arrest him. I want to arrest him personally.'

"I refused. I refused automatically. I was tired and scared, but I refused. But then they put me in a car and showed me that Gestapo automobile waiting for my family. So I said to Blanc: 'O.K. I have a rendezvous with Jacques. I have a rendezvous in a café at two o'clock on Friday.' "

"How about your wife?" I asked.

He answered: "Strangely enough they kept their word; they didn't arrest her that time. She was arrested and held only one day in 1944, later. But she had a friend in the Ministry of the Interior. She helped her."

"And," I asked, "what happened to Jacques?"

Michel looked away from me. He said: "I never saw him again. I never heard from him. His wife was at my trial. She only said the way I had been forced to give away our rendezvous was understandable. She asked the court to understand me and forgive me. She testified that Jacques was sent to Germany and died there. I can imagine how he died."

After he betrayed Jacques, the Nazis sent Dupont back to prison, where he remained until just before the Allies landed in Normandy. During the spring of 1944 he was taken by convoy to a large concentration camp near Compiègne. There he managed to escape in the confusion of unloading. When he got back to Paris he found a friend who told him where his wife was in the countryside. He visited her for a few days. She told him she often saw Mme. Jacques. They had remained good friends.

When he returned to Paris he stayed with an acquaintance near the Porte de Clichy. There he learned of the Allied landing. He and a small group of intimates, none of whom knew he had betrayed Jacques, celebrated the invasion at a gay luncheon. Then he borrowed a bicycle and rode westward toward Normandy.

Whenever he saw German troops he stopped and fraternized with them. They were remarkably friendly and generous with drinks. They kept saying: "Alles ist über." But they didn't seem to mind. By the end of the day, Michel was quite drunk.

When he reached Nogent-le-Rotrou, near Alençon, he found himself at the edge of a forest. He rode through this in the gathering darkness and passed six large gasoline tanks guarded by two Nazi soldiers. He said: "I thought how nice it would be to blow them up. Yet I rode by."

This was the moment, apparently, that massive psychological moment, when Michel Dupont again became a hero. He remembered that, to his own astonishment, he suddenly reflected: "Now I can do something." He found himself talking to himself. He found himself saying: "I can kill Germans again. I can murder these dirty bastards. Maybe I won't bring back Jacques but I'll send him some company." This was not mere patriotism or rage. It was something more: an atavistic return to the ritual of blood sacrifice, the purging of pain in pain.

He turned back. He hid his cycle behind a tree and walked quietly. The two guards were chatting. He could hear their grunted soldier talk. Michel sneaked up in the darkness and opened the tap of a fuel tank. He dribbled a little petrol to the border of the clearing, dropped a match upon it and ran away. The tanks blew up with a formidable, noisy flame.

"I was too stupid then to realize that even in those woods the Germans had telephone wires," Dupont said. "In the light of the flames I saw two or three cars roaring about. Right away they picked me up as a suspect. They took me to the headquarters of their military police. That was in a large house. They didn't seem to have any place to put me so they started questioning me in the back yard, where a soldier stood guard. I just played dumb. And they had lots of other problems.

"Around 10 P.M. I figured I could escape. The soldier was sitting down. He seemed to be sleeping. So I took little pebbles and threw them to see if he was really awake. He wasn't. The wall was only about seven feet high. It was the only chance I had. There was a barrel overturned at the foot. So I suddenly ran and jumped from the barrel over the wall. Once I got to the other side I scrambled away in the underbrush. I hid in a nearby barn."

In the morning a French farmer opened the door. Michel said to him, "Surely you will give me some soup and hide me from the Germans." Then he continued: "The farmer gave me all of that. Lots of soup. While I was there a German came up and asked for my papers. But the farmer said: 'He is one of my laborers.' I looked so dirty that this seemed reasonable. The farmer gave me another bicycle and I went on to Alençon, where I spent two or three days.

"I wanted to go to St. Lô to join the division of Leclerc. Everyone said it was there. However, I couldn't get through. It was already in the battle area. So I stayed on in Alençon and waited for the Yankees."

The first American Michel saw was a captain in the 2nd

Armored Division. Dupont said he knew something of radio transmission. "I need someone like that," said the captain. "See if you can't refresh your memory and stay with us." He remained all the way to Chartres and Rambouillet. There he met Hemingway.

On that day he was driving a truck captured from the Germans, still wearing civilian clothes, with seven German prisoners riding behind. He remembers, after depositing this cargo, stopping by a hotel "and just looking on because there were a lot of American war correspondents." And also Hemingway. He was surrounded by forty or fifty Frenchmen. The American troops were waiting for Leclerc, whose division was slated to enter Paris first. They had been waiting around a long time.

"Hemingway asked me, because I spoke English—I learned it in the film trade—if it was possible to go into Paris. He wanted to get there fast. I said I thought we could try. We started moving on toward Paris. In the Vallée de Chevreuse there was a big batch of Germans on a hilltop. They surrendered and also I got a uniform. I got a uniform from a dead American and I went on into Paris. But Hemingway had driven ahead while I was changing. He was in a hurry.

"I had lost touch with Hemingway. But he had told me he would be at the Ritz, so I started in that direction when I got to Paris. I was stopped by fighting near the Tuileries. I wanted to go on to the Ritz even though I was told it was still full of Germans. So I left my truck very near the Arcades and I got into a scrap with the Germans at the Tuileries. There was a tank from Leclerc's French division

121

and three or four armored cars. But the Germans had ten Tiger tanks. We could do nothing. A few French civilians were there. They were marvelous. Eventually they helped our troops set those tanks on fire."

How often these days we walk by that lovely corner, by the former royal handball court, across from the old Talleyrand mansion, where the child-filled Tuileries Gardens join that spacious Place de la Concorde where French rulers lost their heads before a roaring mob nearly two centuries ago.

I didn't get back to Paris that summer of 1944 until weeks after the fight Michel had described; when the wrecked machinery had been dragged away, the blood washed off the broad pavements, and all that remained were pocks and scars, marking the symmetrical statues, walls and buildings. Yet, if you have ever been pinned down by a tank, cowering into a cliffside, hearing the beehum of splattering machine-gun bullets, watching the shells hit rock above you and whir off incandescent into space, you can imagine that desperate little battle: a few armed soldiers, a few armed civilians, a handful of vehicles and the squat, evil, retreating Nazi beetles.

All that is left today to remind us of that August morning is a series of small bronze plaques set neatly into the wall beneath the Orangerie Museum and, below them, always, fading flowers. Names and dates: Raymond Mestracci, sergent, régiment de marche du Tchad, mort pour la France, le 25 août 1944; Lopez-Ros, soldat de 2ᵉ classe, régiment de marche du Tchad, mort pour la France, le 25 août 1944; Madeleine Brinet, infirmière de la C.R.F., morte pour la

France, le 25 août 1944 . . . Ici est tombé le 25 août 1944, l'adjudant Michel Mouchet, du régiment de sapeurs-pompiers de Paris, mort pour la Libération; Ici Guy Lecomte, F.F.I. du 1ᵉʳ arrondᵗ., est tombé glorieusement le 25 août 1944, agé de 21 ans; Ici Georges Bailly, étudiant en pharmacie, agé de 24 ans, est mort héroïquement pour la France, le 25 août 1944, à la Libération de Paris . . . Ici tomba héroïquement, le 25 août 1944, Marcel Bizien, chef de char, 2ᵉ division blindée, du Général Leclerc, après avoir attaqué et détruit un char tigre allemand.

All these fine young people, men and a woman, dead for France: soldiers and civilians, fireman, nurse, student, some who had fought their way homeward from the elephant-hammered African Chad and others who rushed in from the suburbs to help the liberation, dead and buried beneath the wall of a former royal handball court. But Michel Dupont, the little man toying with death, escaped it.

A Monsieur Brun, an industrialist who knew both Michel and his family and who was, incidentally, the only French civilian brave enough to give Michel a favorable affidavit during his later trial, spoke of this battle, in which he himself had participated, in the formal testimonial he prepared and sent to Dupont's lawyer.

"Although Michel Dupont and I had talked for years about France and what we might do for France," he recalled, "that morning we had the pleasure of capturing between four hundred and five hundred Boche prisoners in the Tuileries. There were only fifteen of us at that moment. Yet, although the Germans may have been resigned to their fate, nevertheless they were still armed."

When it was all over, the smoke still drifting upward in the sunlight, Dupont collected twelve German Schmeisser machine pistols as a gift for Hemingway and made his way, as evening fell, to the luxurious Hotel Ritz, where he had never been before. He found everybody celebrating. The waiters, old customers, new military clients, were gathered in the restaurant, drinking champagne and brandy. "It was very gay," Michel recalls. "For a moment I felt like a new man, a happy man. For a moment I really lost my memories."

Next morning Dupont went to the Rue St. Didier to sign up with the French Army. There was too much confusion and too many volunteers. His application was turned down. Consequently he decided he would stay on with Hemingway, who took him on as a permanent driver. After a few days, reunited with his wife, he drove his new boss to Soissons and joined the 4th Division, where General (then Colonel) Lanham was commanding the 22nd Infantry Regiment.

"Those weeks," he said, "were splendid. Hemingway was really a great fighter. Certainly that. He never wanted to stay at headquarters. He would always tell me to keep my jeep ready so we could move on one second's notice."

One spring afternoon, as the war was ending, Hemingway patted Michel on the back and told him to return to Paris and find himself a job. He was wearing an American uniform. However, he wasn't in anybody's army so he didn't have to wait for the red tape of demobilization. He simply said good-by and went on home.

Michel wasn't sure quite what to do. There was no movie

industry. He had had his fill of chicken farming. At one time, early during the occupation, he had learned something about making women's shoes; so he started to make shoes again. He and his cousin set up a little shop near the Etoile.

In the middle of the night on September 20, 1945, as he was returning from work after laying out new patterns for winter models, he arrived at the modest apartment he had rented in the suburbs. His wife and children—he had had a second child in February, 1945—were out, visiting his mother. Instead, he discovered four French inspectors from the Défense Secrète du Territoire. They regarded him with stony faces.

First they asked for his identity papers. Then they questioned him for a while. Finally they took him back to the Rue des Saussaies. They said to him: "You already know this place?" He answered sadly: "Yes."

He was locked up in a cellar with forty other men. He wasn't able to sleep; and in the morning a thorough interrogation started. The police beat him and, in the intervening pauses, asked questions about Jacques and Blanc.

I inquired once: "Did they beat you as badly as the Germans had?"

"Yes," he answered. "It was just as bad. They took the roller out of a typewriter and with that they beat my feet and legs and they also beat me on my privates. They tried to make me confess all kinds of things I hadn't done. This lasted for many hours. And then, quite suddenly, they confronted me with Blanc. How surprised I was to see him. He looked at me coldly, something like a turtle."

Dupont was kept in prison for three and a half years before his final trial. The state judge appointed an attorney to defend him. This lawyer recommended that he should appear together with Blanc. "Ah," he recalled, "that was a great mistake. I was sentenced to fifteen years in prison. Blanc, however, and I say this with no regret, was shot."

Michel's mother visited the judge after sentence was passed. The judge admitted he had been severe, perhaps too severe, and promised to seek reduction of the sentence. He said he recognized Michel had been more victim than accomplice. Nevertheless he was sent to a state prison where for one year he was assigned to making baby carriages. He found this difficult. "The food was terrible," he remembered. "There was no running water. Accommodation was awful. All of us were political prisoners. Yes, we were all collaborators.

"After a year I was transferred to another place near Saumur, where we made blankets, and it was a little better. And the judge kept his promise to my mother. My sentence was reduced to six years. I left jail May 9, 1951."

I didn't have a chance to finish asking all my questions because I was called away to Eastern Europe on a trip. Dupont kept in touch with me, however, and sent a series of pathetic letters explaining how one attempt after another to find work had failed. When I returned to Paris I invited him around for lunch one day. He ate sparingly and timidly. He kept looking at his plate. Finally, with considerable embarrassment, he asked for a small loan.

"What are you going to do?" I inquired. "Is it wholly impossible to find some sort of job?"

Michel replied: "You just don't see what's going on. I can't work any more in the movies as I am 'an unworthy national' according to the law. I have no legal rights. I can't vote in elections. I have this burden to bear all the rest of my life. And people won't hire me."

"But surely some of your friends have remained loyal?"

"Some, perhaps. But they are always afraid I may ask them for a thousand francs."

"And those who were in the resistance with you?"

"They let me down completely.

"I have nothing," said Dupont. "They are making me a beggar. My mother is near Toulouse at the home of one of my cousins. But there is nothing for me there, nothing for me to do. I went to Paris looking for work. I went to Lille looking for work. In Lille, there was someone I knew in the textile business. But he is a former officer. He said he couldn't take on a 'collabo'; he would get into all sorts of trouble. And twice I got jobs in little factories. When the unions found that I had been in prison, and what I had been in prison for, they struck. I had to leave.

"Now I live on nothing except what little help I get from people like you. And my mother has to work. My mother never worked in her life. We came from the middle class. She was a protected woman. She didn't know what it was to work. Today, when she is sixty-five years old, she has to work, because I can't support her and she gets no insurance from the state."

There are, unhappily, some people predestined to misfortune. Certain religions deal with this tragic circumstance. Calvinism has its built-in rationalization of such an evil fate.

It blames the individual as well as his cursed heritage. But I wonder if it takes account of the helpless pawns like Michel Dupont. Buddhism and Hinduism have their curious cycles of incarnation and reincarnation in one or another form. But Michel had been a Catholic. And long since he had lost touch with faith in anything—human or divine.

It was only in the autumn of 1951 that I had a chance to finish study the policedossier on the Michel Dupont case, sent on with the help of my friend Tillion. And what a miracle of bureaucracy: there, tidily, as if there had never been a war, defeat, occupation or victory, were the cold, statistical facts set out, amended and perhaps re-amended by anonymous agents; Lord knows, some among them must have collaborated well with Nazi colleagues to keep their files so complete through chaos. Here are the salient facts (with names and certain dates disguised for Michel's sake):

JACQUES

According to a memorandum from the Fourth Section of the Judiciary Police Services, Jacques had the following inscribed in his folder:

"He is known to the police as a militant of the ex-Communist party. He drew attention to himself from 1928 on when he was a member of the national committee of the Friends of the U.S.S.R. This same organization put him in charge of organizing and directing a cultural project.

"For this purpose he often spoke at meetings and reunions. In 1927 he declared himself publicly as a sympathizer with Communist theories.

"Upon the conclusion of the German-Russian pact in

August, 1939, he is said to have remained an ardent admirer of Moscow's doctrines."

There is the following significant note added by the French police during the occupation period:

"Please erase Jacques from the list of illegal personalities established by the Prefecture of Police. Jacques has just been excluded from the Communist Party for having long ago ceased all political activity and for disapproving the party line."

And a curt postwar footnote:

"Jacques was arrested by the Gestapo in 1943 and deported to Germany, where he died in the Bergen-Belsen camp.

"He had been betrayed by a certain Dupont."

BLANC

"In 1933 Blanc joined the Free Masons and became affiliated to the Jaune Lodge, where he rose to the rank of 'venerable.' He remained a Free Mason until the society was dissolved by Vichy government legislation.

"His activity under the occupation was notable, above all for his considerable aid to the Germans.

"From July, 1941, he attacked the parliamentary regime, Jewry and the Free Masons, all of whom he held responsible for the defeat.

"In the summer of 1941 the Germans decided to make use of his abilities and they made him an S.S. officer in charge of the anti-Free Mason forces in France.

"From that time on until the liberation he became an ever more valuable auxiliary of the German intelligence services in the Hotel Lutétia. He had an office and a secretary and received a monthly salary of 6,000 francs. He handled confidential political investigations of interest to the German police. He moved throughout all of France in both the free zone and the occupied zone. He even traveled abroad, especially in Switzerland.

"In July, 1942, he went to Lyon and introduced himself as a 'venerable,' well known by other Masons. By this means he contacted a certain Monsieur du Moulin, who gave him the address of an editor of a clandestine newspaper. Both du Moulin and the editor were arrested and deported.

"During the winter of 1943, by accident, Blanc and his secretary met a certain Dupont in a bar where Gaullists used to gather. Dupont, who was drunk, boasted of possessing arms as well as of aiding the resistance movement. He also mentioned a Monsieur Jacques who was hiding in Paris because of his activity in the resistance and the Communist party.

"A few days later Dupont was arrested by the Gestapo. He was induced to give all useful help with the intention of having Jacques arrested.

"Four days later [ah, what a sadness lies between] Dupont saw Jacques again at a rendezvous with him in a café. It was at this meeting that Jacques was arrested by the German police and deported to Germany. He died there in the Bergen-Belsen camp.

"In December, 1943, Blanc went to Bordeaux and presented himself as a member of the resistance to the Countess A. She put him in touch with a certain B., a leading resistant. B. was arrested by the Gestapo. A few months later, on the orders of the German Sicherheitsdienst, Blanc was active in the Chambéry region where he caused many resistance members to be arrested.

"Still later many persons were arrested in Hasparren as a result of his activity.

"During July 1944, Blanc was ordered to infiltrate the resistance network of Clamart. His infiltration led to the arrest of many persons.

"Blanc was condemned to death by a sentence pronounced by the 7th sub-section of the court of justice on December 24, 1948. He was executed March 29, 1949, in the courtyard of the Montrouge Fort at Arcueil.

Dupont

"Although he never attracted attention to himself for his political views or drew the attention of the police, Dupont had often expressed his antipathy toward the occupation troops and the (Vichy) French government. Moreover, he was arrested for drunkenness and insulting the chief of state (Pétain) in November, 1941. But the only charge leveled against him was that of insulting a policeman, for which he was sentenced to fifteen days in prison with suspended sentence and two hundred francs fine on December 22, 1941.

"Early during the war he was taken into custody for breaking a Nazi decree calling for the declaration of all persons of Jewish faith (his wife being an Israelite). A little later he was arrested by the economic police of the occupation for illegal manufacture and sale of shoes and illegal price raising."

According to the police records, "Dupont, who was drunk, boasted in a bar to the German agent, Blanc, of possessing arms and of provisioning the insurgents. He also indiscreetly mentioned that Jacques was hiding in Paris because of his activity in the resistance and in the Communist party.

"A few days later Dupont was arrested by the Gestapo and, after questioning, promised he would give all useful indications with a view to the arrest of Jacques. Dupont saw Jacques again at a rendezvous with him in a café. There Jacques was arrested by the German police and deported to Germany where he died in the Bergen-Belsen camp."

The following footnote was added after the war: "Dupont was sentenced to three months in September, 1945, for robbery. In 1948 he was sentenced to fifteen years forced labor for collaborating with the enemy."

Attached to this dossier were testimonials. The first, dated February, 1946, from the colonel of his 1939 regiment, said: "Dupont's dash, courage, spirit of discipline and absolute contempt for danger attracted immediate attention during the Warndt Forest combats in which his unit was engaged in October-November. He was one of the first to volunteer for duty in the newly-created guerrilla corps (Corps Franc) of his battalion. He participated in all dangerous missions. His bravery and coolness aroused the admiration of all those around him. During the fighting he performed his duty with self-denial and courage."

His former sergeant major added: "Dupont's bravery was exemplary. He volunteered for all reconnaissance missions and always did his duty to my entire satisfaction."

And there was the testimonial from Hemingway, drawn up as always from Finca Vigia, San Francisco de Paula, Cuba, on Christmas Eve, 1945, which said in part:

"Dupont worked with the French volunteers who, under the command of Col. D. K. E. Bruce [later United States Ambassador to France, Germany and Britain] of the American Army OSS, gathered information on German troop dispositions and their defensive positions prior to the French 2nd Armored Division's advance on Paris.

"Michel Dupont carried out greatly useful reconnaissance missions with much courage and bravery. The officers of the American 4th Infantry Division often praised him for his bravery, his zeal and his intelligence.

"All Americans who were in contact with him knew of his anti-Nazi and anti-German sentiments which were confirmed time and time again by his acts during one of the most difficult periods of the war."

The above was duly notarized by the U.S. Vice Consul at Havana.

Another statement, signed by General Lanham, certified to "The following facts":

"Dupont was among the first to cross the German border. He joined the advance elements of my regiment. He exposed himself numerous times to enemy fire. His courage and composure under fire were an example to all of us. His conduct under fire was remarkable and widely commented on. Once, Dupont volunteered to go with a team commanded by Captain Whaley of the 22nd Infantry which was counterattacking the German forces in that sector. Dupont fought as a rifleman with that unit all day long. The officers of this particular outfit personally praised him for his valor on the battlefield, his composure under fire and the ardor of his attacks against a desperately determined enemy.

"Always as a volunteer, Dupont served as Mr. Hemingway's bodyguard during the whole campaign. He was constantly on the dangerous paths and roads of the Hürtgen Forest at all hours of the day and night. One after the other, all officers and men who were under my command commented at different times on Dupont's bravery and his hatred of the Germans. I cannot say personally how many Germans he killed. But according to the first-hand reports of my men, I know he killed many. I have never known a man who hated the Germans as much as Dupont or who fought them with so much spirit.

"If Monsieur Dupont had been an American soldier instead of a French volunteer combating as an irregular, I would have cited him personally for his bravery in combat. Other officers in my regiment who saw him fight the Germans would also have cited him for valor. But since he was not a member of the army of the United States, and he was fighting as an irregular, I was unable to cite him officially for his valiant conduct."

And, finally, the police file contained an extraordinary letter from M. Brun, the industrialist, to Michel Dupont's lawyer. This said in part:

"Let me introduce myself and give my references. I am at your disposition. My family has been in industry for four generations. Among banking and business circles it possesses a reputation which I believe is well established and which I try to maintain.

"Michel Dupont was a loyal friend whom I especially enjoyed seeing since we arrived at the same opinions although along different roads, not being employed in the same kind of work or enjoying the same friends or education. Yet we understood each other on the grounds of patriotism and devotion to our families.

"I can say that Michel Dupont is deeply patriotic although his love of adventure may at times have led him to fail in his duty. I can also say that the love Michel bears toward his family, toward his wife, is his great reason for living.

"Michel's temperament led him to take risks, and although I can say on my honor that I have never seen him drunk with my own eyes, the places and people he frequented were not to my taste. This was the Michel Dupont whom I did not know.

"Others aside from myself will testify as to what Michel Dupont did following the liberation of Paris. Let me add that the Americans whom I later met and who knew him were profoundly convinced of his bravery, of his heroism. Without being bombastic, one can say that to the Americans, in the American Army where he accompanied Hemingway (thus drawing considerable attention to himself), he represented France with all her panache.

"But we still have the denunciation to deal with.

"Michel spent the first years of the German occupation in the country as discreetly as possible. His military history and his wife's racial background made him too vulnerable. This he knew full well.

"He came out of retirement because of his love of adventure and of risk. Then the catastrophe arrived. He was imprisoned by the Germans. . . .

"His wife, his daughter!

"What terrible moral pressure those who know this man's instability and his love for those two beings were able to exert!

"His wife! His daughter!"

When Michel was tried in 1948 he received scant sympathy from the press. One paper wrote: "In the dock is another accused man, one Michel Dupont, a Resistant who, when arrested, under pressure denounced an unfortunate man who was deported and never returned."

Another said of him: "As for Dupont, the disconsolate helper of Blanc—and his victim—the judges understood that cowardice born of fear had led to his complicity."

He was sentenced to fifteen years forced labor and national degradation. Application for pardon was refused. An eye-witness newspaper reporter at the trial observed: "As for Dupont, on hearing his sentence of fifteen years at forced labor pronounced, he wept like a child."

The last time I ever saw Michel was late in 1951 when, one mid-afternoon, he dropped in with a weary hang-dog look. Things had been going just as badly. He had a temporary, part-time job as a waiter. His boss asked no questions because he needed a substitute and Michel was willing to work at a cut rate.

I gave him a drink and a cigarette. "How on earth," I asked, "do you manage to keep your wife and kids these days? I know your mother supports herself. But your second baby was born just before you went to jail in 1945; how can you feed four mouths?"

"I guess I never told you this," he said. "I guess I was ashamed. But that's one worry I no longer have. You see, my wife let me down. When they sentenced me and confiscated all my rights, she decided to divorce me. She married a friend of mine from the resistance. They run a shop together. And they have the children; I never see them. I never saw her since. That is the woman I went to Hell and back for."

There isn't much to add: the slightly bibulous little man who enjoyed the bar-fringes of lower-middle-class society; his frightened wife and helpless baby; the former Communist, betrayed and gassed in Belsen; the jealous traitor who wanted personally to arrest him. The strange, undramatic, tawdry end: desertion by his wife, the one being, the one symbol, that had kept him going; Michel Dupont, so utterly alone, an authentic hero of two campaigns, 1939 and 1944–45, undecorated, unrecognized, unadmitted and reviled; no longer in any man's army or in any man's society: an outcast, without friends, without family, without faith; he even abandoned his religion. Driven to the verge of petty crime, inclined to drink; by law a traitor, by fact indiscreet, frequently foolish; yet, nevertheless, a man, a brave man, excluded as unworthy by what we call society and granted no chance to achieve redemption.

All of us dwell inherently alone, cut off from each other's souls by impenetrable plate-glass windows. But, my God, how alone that man was, isolated even from the memory of his courage, nothing to look forward to and everything to forget!

One day, in December, 1951, I played golf with General Eisenhower at Morfontaine, near Paris. It was the weekday when the club normally was closed but they opened the course for their distinguished guest.

We lunched alone in the little dining room and began to talk about the war. The future President was complaining about the slowness of Montgomery in closing the Falaise Gap during the Normandy campaign. He said Monty's excessive caution had allowed too many Germans to escape the "killing ground." I asked him to elucidate, so he got up, collected a lot of salt and pepper cellars (the allies were the salt, the Nazis were the pepper) and moved them around on the table top. The table "cloth" was of paper; so he drew battle lines with a pencil I provided. Later he showed on another table how he would have fought Monty's great battle of Alamein.

We rode home toward Paris in his huge black car, a Secret Service representative sitting beside the driver and a little Renault loaded with French security men whizzing along behind. We talked about war in general and we talked about war in particular and then we talked about what war did to individual human beings.

At that point I said: "I'd like to ask you three questions,

all together. What does a man deserve from his country if he is an acknowledged hero? What does a man deserve if he is a collaborator with the enemy? And what does a man deserve if he is both?"

General Ike looked puzzled. He scratched his jaw and his face took on a rather endearing expression of bewilderment. "Now what are you getting at?" he inquired. So I told him the story of Michel Dupont. I told it to him in great detail and he listened in silence.

When I had finished, he looked out at the encroaching darkness, already beginning to obscure Paris' ugly northern suburbs. "Well, I'll be damned," he said. "I'll be damned."

Michel Dupont was.

LETTRE D'ENVOI

In 1954, Dupont wrote me what proved to be a farewell letter, couched in his imperfect English. I reproduce it faithfully.

"Here is some more to add to Mike's story.

"The last time I saw you in 1951, in Paris, I was going to Geneva, where I thought I could find a job. I didn't had no luck there and, coming back to Paris, I was obliged, being broke, to take another job as a waiter in a café. I staid there for 3 months, as I only had a replacement job.

"Then, I started working for a still picture firm, selling enlargements. They sent me up to Lille. It was a distasteful job, knowing I was cheating the people on what I was selling them. Anyway, I made a living out of it.

"During this time, I met one of my former friend, whom I was in reclusion with. He introduced me to his family, which owned a garage in Le Bourget, Paris. Everytimes I was going back to Paris, I would go to them and stay with them a couple of days or so. My friend had a sister of about my age. We came to like each other. And I married her. Yes, Mike has some luck. I now have wife again. And she has children, from before.

"One evening, we were having supper with some friends, and we decided to go out to have a drink before going to bed. Our friends had a small Renault, too small to contain all of us. My wife had her car all the way down the garage, and blocked by all the customers' cars. She decided to take the car of one of the customers, whom she did know very well, intending to tell him the next morning, and being sure he wouldn't mind it, for she had borrowed his car many times. So we took off, and luck being on my side, we had a crash. The car was all wrecked up. She didn't had nothing. I got out of it with a cut in my scalp. They fixed me up at the hospital. But, having no license for the car, we were taken to the police station, where we staid till the next morning. Everything cleared up then, when the owner of the car told the police he did loan us the car and just forgot to give us the license for it. Later on, he decided to sue the garage for this action, asking a new car and indemnity for the time he would be without a car.

"The parents of my friends were out in the country for the week-end. We were all upset and scared of what they would say. We decided to leave Paris, leaving to my friend the charge of telling his parents and try to smooth up everything for us. He would let us know when everything would

be fixed and the time for us to come back. So we went to
Lille, and I continued my work there. Pretty soon, they sent
me down to Rouen. I started my work there, but it was not
half as good as Lille, and now, we were two to live on the
job. In Rouen, I met a lot of GIs, and became acquainted
with a bar owner, who offered me to work for him and take
care of the American customers. This job was better and I
jumped on the occasion. I started saving whatever I could.

"One GI whom I knew very well had his wife with him.
They were living in a small town where all the Army is
stationed. He talked to me into opening up a place for the
GIs and their dependents only. I jumped on the idea. I
found a shop which was to rent, big enough to put a bar
and restaurant room in it.

"At the time, we had 75,000 francs in front of us, not
much to put up a place. Anyway, I started on it, buying
wood, nails, paint, and so on. . . . In a week, I built up
the bar, the tables, fixed all the electricity, did the painting,
and 15 days after, we were ready to operate, having bought
a license (beer and wine) for the place.

"We called it the Mike's, and pretty soon, the place was
crowded. We had good trade during the week-time, and on
Saturday and Sunday, we had American bands and dance,
singers and so on. . . . Everybody was delighted by the
place, specially because they were sure to be among themselves, with people talking English. For my wife talks English, and my step-daughter, who came down for her vacation,
does too. But the French people didn't like it too much.
They started by breaking the front-glasses at night-time.

I complained to the police, but they didn't wanted to do anything about it, and, on the contrary, they started to give me trouble.

"We were allowed to stay opened till 2 o'clock in the morning till the end of August. From then, only till midnight everyday during the week-time. It was O.K., but on Saturday and Sunday, specially by the beginning of the month, that was a little short. You know how GIs are when they have money. Just to tell you, during October, they fined me 12 times for being opened late. The latest they caught me was 6 minutes past 12. Before, they tried to charge me with everything—having special women working in the place, gambling, selling drinks to people already drunk. They never could get me on those charges, for the good reason that they couldn't ever find anything wrong in my place.

"Nevertheless, by the end of November, they closed me up for 3 months, on the charge of the 12 times being opened late. So, broken hearted, we had to close. We came to Paris, to see my new family-in-law. A few days after our arrival, we found out that my brother-in-law, who was taking care of the garage—my father-in-law being too old for it—had made some bad business, and was so far in debt that the only way to settle everything was to sell the garage. I worked on that job for 2 months, and finally sold it for 8 million francs, of which very little was left on account of all my brother-in-law's debts.

"Anyway, my father-in-law gave us 1,700,000 francs to start a new business, and we decided to invest them in an automatic laundry in la Rochelle.

"I found a place, an old garage well situated in the center of the town, and bought it for 1,000,000 francs, 600,000 cash. I ordered 5 machines, paid 250,000 down, and started to fix the place up. I had to remake the ceiling, the floor, the walls. I did. Then put a front to the place instead of the old wooden door, fix up the electricity, build up a counter, fix up the plumbing. Everything is done now. I am still waiting for the electric meter to be put in. I have to do the painting, finish the plumbing, put some linoleum tiles on the floor, and I'll be ready to wash the dirty clothes of whoever will trust me to wash them.

"As you see, I have been in a lot of troubles, working like a slave all the time. I wouldn't care for me, that's the men's share in life. But my wife had to do the same to see us through so far, and I wish I could get a little bit ahead and let her rest a little. I can't say I am unlucky, for I fell on the most understanding and courageous woman there's on earth. I do hope in 15 days from now we will be able to start to work. We have been working on the place since the 15th of March and living on just enough to keep us alive so we could invest everything we had in the business. Of course, I am very deep in debt. I know that, as soon as I open, I'll have something real. I'll be able to draw figures, and make schedule for the payment. For the time, I'm just trying to pull it through. I've got to succeed, because now, I'll have to take care of us first, then my father and mother-in-law, and my mother and my aunt.

"Everything would be O.K. I don't want to get rich in a day or even in 10 years. All I want out of this d . . . . life is to make everything comfortable for my folks and enjoy a decent life. The trouble is I am getting sicker and sicker. I must have an ulcer. Lots of time, I am suffering so much it take all my strength away. Still I need a lot to see it through.

"Be sure I'll always be your respectful. Mike."

These are the words of the Resistentialist, the courageous coward, who knows he is defeated and yet refuses to yield: "That's the men's share in life. . . . I can't say I am unlucky." For Dupont and for his fellow Resistentialists Vladimir Dedijer and the Ripper, everything in the end failed except self; yet each, in his way, discovered that, without cause, without country, without creed, without credo, they could stand obstinate and still, when needed, be malleable, hearing outside them and around them the loud plangency of uncontrollable storms, taking part in terror and resisting terror. They had within them the ability to walk the hard, stony way, unbent and alone.

CHAPTER 3

CHILD OF THE REVOLUTION

"Whatever occurs, I am not going to eat dirt. If you have to eat dirt once in your life you will have to say it is good forever."
—VLADIMIR DEDIJER

"We have had reason to fear," said Pierre Victurnien Vergniaud, a fiery eighteenth-century Girondist, "that the revolution, like Saturn, would devour in succession all her children." Shortly after that, accused by Robespierre, he laid his head on the guillotine's bloody board.

One by one, the Terror gnawed its offspring: Marat, Brissot, Gensonné, Danton, Desmoulins, Hébert; Fouquier-Tinville, Herman; until the day came for great Robespierre himself. His wounds bound up, bumping indifferent in a tumbril through the roaring crowd, he arrived before that tall cruel instrument known as the Widow, erected in what is now the Place de la Concorde. The executioner tore off his bandages, wrenching a single scream of agony from his stony silence. And the blade fell. "The executioner held up the head that the mob might look for the last time on the man who had canonized its virtues and been blind to its faults."

The Saturnic law is the law of revolution and we in our own times have seen it immutably apply—in the sanguinary Russian purge trials, where loyal Communists were induced by some strange means to condemn themselves, and in the furious epuration of Titoists and Revisionists in Eastern Europe.

I have known many victims of this revolutionary greed for its own kin. And of all these perhaps the strangest case was George Andreitchin's. George Andreitchin was the son of Bulgarian peasants in that mountainous southland where, in summer, below every peak, the valleys are filled with roses—a crop for perfume makers in distant well-to-do countries.

In order to popularize himself with his subjects early this century, King Ferdinand of Bulgaria decided to adopt several peasant lads. These were chosen from all over the country by schoolteachers and George was selected from his district. Together with the other youngsters, he was educated in Sofia and lived in the palace as a son of the ruler, becoming Ferdinand's favorite.

In those days the Balkans were in perpetual ferment. Strange nationalist, anarchist and Marxist movements simmered through the backward nations and young Andreitchin was caught up in the current. One day, when he was just seventeen, the King summoned him and said:

"George, my police are telling me things about you. I hear rumors that you are a Socialist." Andreitchin replied: "No, Your Majesty. I am an anarchist." Ferdinand said: "I am sorry, my boy, I will give you twenty-four hours, twenty-four hours to get away before my police begin to move."

George left Bulgaria just before the First Great War and made his way to the United States. There he became a labor organizer for the International Workers of the World, the old I.W.W., a romantic syndicalism that cynically advised impoverished laboring men: "When you die there'll be pie in the sky." William Bullitt, later our first Ambassador to the Soviet Union, at that time a great liberal, became interested in George. When the young Bulgarian was sentenced to prison in the early 1920's, Bullitt provided bail and Andreitchin skipped the country.

George headed for Russia to join Leon Trotsky, whom he had known in New York. He worked his passage over the Atlantic and started across the Continent by train. He was in a third-class railway carriage, rattling through newly-born Czechoslovakia, when, at a rural station, an old man with a beard, a shotgun and a hunter's bag entered his compartment and sat down.

The two stared for a moment—and fell into each other's arms. It was Ferdinand. "George," said the old man with great emotion. "Yes, Your Majesty," Andreitchin replied. The exiled king forgot his day's shooting plans and rode for hours beside his adopted son, discussing the future and the past.

When he reached Moscow, Andreitchin became Trotsky's private secretary. He helped the fiery revolutionist with his speeches and traversed the Russian steppes with him in a lurching armored train. But the time came for the Saturnic law to apply its appetite.

Trotsky, leaving Andreitchin behind in the Soviet Union, fled, first to Turkey, then to Mexico, where he was finally murdered by one of Stalin's henchmen. George was arrested and taken to the infamous Lubyanka Prison. After many weeks of solitary confinement, he was summoned before an interrogator, a cold, dispassionate secret police official, who said to him: "Citizen"—not "Comrade," the polite form among good Bolshevik colleagues—"We offer you a choice. You are going to be charged, but it is up to you to decide whether to plead guilty as a Trotskyite or as an American spy. Which do you accept?"

Either admission would, of course, be perilous. George, on orders from Maxim Litvinov, the Foreign Commissar, had been seeing much of the Americans. He had also been one of Trotsky's closest friends. "I guess," he replied, "you had better list me as a Trotskyite."

He was sent to a prison camp in the far north, where he remained for years, cutting timber. Some months after Germany attacked Russia in 1941, George was called in by the camp supervisor, who told him: "We have orders to send you to Moscow." Andreitchin didn't know whether this implied his freedom or his death.

The transportation system near the Finnish border had broken down so Andreitchin and a handful of other prisoners, accompanied by guards, had to walk many miles through the heavy autumnal snows. Each night they huddled about fires together with their "protectors." When they finally reached a northern rail junction, they were herded into freight cars bound for the capital, where, on arrival, George was incarcerated again in the Lubyanka.

After four days, he was summoned by the commandant, nattily uniformed and most agreeable, who invited him to sit down, offered him one of those long Russian *papirossi* and said: "Comrade"—what an improvement over "Citizen"—"I am afraid we have lost your records. I am unfamiliar with your case. Can you tell me why you are under sentence?" George thought for a moment and then said: "I think it is because I was suspected of being pro-American."

He was returned to his cell. But the next day he received a clean suit of clothes. A barber came in to shave him and cut his hair, he was bathed, manicured and served the first of a series of nourishing meals. He was given books and newspapers in which he read about the "great, patriotic" war with Germany, that England was now Russia's ally and America an active friend. A fortnight later a colonel in the secret police called for him and said: "Comrade Andreitchin, we are taking you home."

Outside, a Zis limousine was waiting. The colonel asked George to enter the automobile first and instructed the chauffeur to drive around Moscow while he pointed out changes and improvements "since you were here." Finally, they arrived before a modest, dreary house. The colonel led the way up two flights of stairs, knocked upon a door and it was opened—by George's wife.

That was October, 1941. The Nazis were on the outskirts of Moscow, right up to the Khimki water tower. Therefore, when Stalin decided to evacuate Soviet and Comintern officials to Kuibyshev, the temporary diplomatic capital, George, once again a "contact" with the Americans, was sent along.

After the war Andreitchin, always a loyal Communist,

was sent to Bulgaria to help make it a docile satellite. He became counselor to Vassil Kolarov, later the puppet Prime Minister in Sofia and former head of the Comintern. In 1946 the two men invited me to lunch in Paris during the conference in which the victorious allies arranged peace treaties with Hitler's junior Axis partners.

I had just returned from Athens, where my son was born, so George proposed we should drink a toast to him. Kolarov asked his name and I replied, mischievously (the boy was called David), "Basil—Basil the Bulgar slayer." Basil the Bulgar slayer was, for the Greeks, the most famous of all emperors of Byzantium. He captured a Bulgarian army, blinded ninety-nine of each hundred captives, left one eye in the head of every hundredth man, chained them together and marched them home. The Bulgarian Czar committed suicide.

Kolarov, pale with anger, put his glass down, but Andreitchin burst into laughter. Next day he sent me an enormous box of expensive Sobranje cigarettes together with a card: "In honor of Emperor Basil."

As the years went on I began to hear rumors that Andreitchin was again in trouble, this time as a "Titoist." When I returned to Sofia in 1956 I asked an old friend: "And what about Andreitchin? I used to know him in Russia." There was an embarrassed hush, a pause. Finally, I was told: "We have reason to think he is dead. He was sent to a camp near Plovdiv but we heard he died there. You know, he once was in Soviet prison. His health was bad and he was no longer young."

The next day I visited the massive Red Square-style mausoleum that honors another and most redoubtable Bulgarian, Georgi Dimitrov, the man who made a fool of the Nazis during the Reichstag fire trial. This edifice dominates the heart of Sofia as ancient Pharaonic tombs once did Thebes. Dimitrov, in approved Soviet mortuary style, was stuffed and pickled under glass. Next to this grand display was a modest pot containing the choleric Kolarov's ashes. Where George's bones or ashes are I do not know.

This revolutionary cannibalism affected many men besides Andreitchin. One among them was my oldest and dearest Communist friend, who, because he was a Resistentialist, survived—but not without paying a dreadful human sacrifice to the revolution's appetite.

Across the foothills from Bulgaria, where George died, is Yugoslavia, the land of the South Slavs, a country dominated by the fiercely original and independent-minded Serbs.

When I first visited Yugoslavia in 1938, as a very young man, I came to know a group of Serbian youngsters. I often met them in the Triglav, a small, shabby café named for the country's highest mountain. Here we drank wine or powerful plum brandy, shattering our glasses (as was the custom) on the walls or floor. We ate *chevapchichi*, the peppery little Serbian hamburgers, and listened to gypsy girls singing and playing tambourines to the accompaniment of accordions and violins.

In this group was a bulky twenty-four-year-old intellectual named Vladimir Dedijer. Dedijer, a former newsman, had been discharged from his paper because its editors didn't

like his politics, which were very far to the left. In my innocence at the time I didn't know just how far to the left
they were. In fact, Vladimir had just become a member of
the secret Yugoslav Communist party; and so were all his
colleagues in the Triglav. Vlado, as Dedijer was called, had
a young wife and baby and earned his living by translating
into Serbian the writings of Pearl Buck.

Dedijer was and is an impressive physical specimen:
somewhat over six feet tall and weighing about 225 pounds
—hard flesh, bone and muscle. No one could mistake him
for anything but a Serb although he came from the border-
land province of Herzegovina. His face was almost concave,
dish-shaped. It was a face only Serbs seem blessed or cursed
with, a powerful and obstinate face with jutting jaw and
brow. He was a fine athlete and the only one among us
who never smoked or drank even a glass of wine. The others
were named Ivan Ribar, Jr. (known as Lola), Mira Popora
and Slobodan Princip. Princip was a nephew of that famous
Bosnian patriot whose assassination of Archduke Ferdinand
set the world ablaze in 1914.

Occasionally we gathered in Vlado's home, across the
river from Belgrade in the suburb of Zemun. There Dedijer's handsome wife, Olga, the daughter of a former Cabinet Minister, a tall, graceful, black-haired, white-skinned
girl with the features of an ikon saint, sometimes prepared
American flapjacks. Her husband had acquired a taste for
these during a trip to the United States when his brother
Steve was a Princeton undergraduate and rowed on the
university crew.

These young people used to discuss what they would do

in the event of war—an increasing likelihood after Hitler engulfed neighboring Austria and Yugoslavia's ally, Czechoslovakia. They formed a small organization called the Anti-Fascist Youth Movement for the Defense of the Country —an organization made up of university students, patriotic societies and Boy Scouts. They occasionally engaged in simple drills on the hills near Belgrade, mustering a few rifles provided by sympathetic officers. I did not realize until much later that the heart of the group was a disciplined cadre of Communists, including those very men with whom I used to meet.

Before World War II Yugoslavia was a kingdom headed by a vigorously anti-Communist Prince Regent who had strong sympathies with the former Russian Czars and still gave diplomatic recognition to the last Czarist Minister to Belgrade. There were many White Russian refugees in the secret police. Communists, who were banned but retained an underground organization, got short shrift when they were caught. One of their heroes, arrested by the ruthless secret police, goaded them by yelling in his cell: "Come on, torture me: I'll know how to torture you when we come to power."

Dedijer and his young friends therefore ran great risk by joining the conspiratorial movement. Yet they had faith in its aims and Vlado later wrote in a book of his called *The Beloved Land:*

"I was sure that the Yugoslav Revolution would not devour its children. . . . When I said this, I firmly believed that it was the truth, since the children of this revolution are honest."

He had been introduced into the Communist party by a recent graduate of Belgrade University named Milovan Djilas. But, at the time I first knew Dedijer and his friends, Djilas was in prison and I did not meet him. Of the others, the earnest group of youngsters with whom I talked and drank in the grimy Triglav, all save Dedijer are now dead.

Princip died of wounds and typhus late in 1943 while commanding Tito's Partisan armies in East Bosnia. He was a fine, tall, thin, sharp-eyed fellow with a head of long hair. He had a great record for bravery and his name was magic. In that wide region where his uncle, the slayer of Archduke Ferdinand, was revered as a sainted martyr, thousands of peasants joined the Partisans, without respect to ideology, merely when word was sent about that "Princip is here again."

Popora was captured by Mihailovitch's Chetniks, with whom the Partisans fought a bloody private civil war. They turned him over to the Italians, who shot him. He died courageous and stiff-backed, shouting: "Long live the fatherland."

Lola Ribar, a colonel on Tito's general staff, was killed by a German bomb in November, 1943. With him died two British liaison officers. Ribar, as I discovered later, was a member of the Yugoslav Politburo. His father became president of Tito's first parliament.

These youngsters and others like them were Communists who had been organized into disciplined cadres by a Croatian metalworker named Josip Broz, now known to the world as Marshal Tito, leader of World War II's most suc-

cessful guerrilla movement, today President of Yugoslavia
and famous for his rebellion against Stalin.

They hardly knew who Tito was in the prewar days, although all of them had met him at one time or another
and Dedijer had even concealed him occasionally in his
house as an *ilegalac*, an illegal party member. But when
Hitler attacked and overran Yugoslavia in 1941, Tito pulled
together his Communist cells and prepared them for a military uprising.

Dedijer had volunteered into the Royal Yugoslav Army.
However, this collapsed before he could begin to fight, so
he returned to his home near Belgrade to await party instructions. He and a few other soldiers hid their weapons
and Vlado worked in a vineyard.

The Nazi occupation was exceptionally brutal. Gypsies
and Jews were rounded up and gassed to death in grim S.S.
trucks rumbling toward cemeteries. Patriots were hanged
from lampposts in Belgrade. Nevertheless, at the end of
April, 1941, Tito came to the wrecked capital, established
his clandestine high command and waited for Moscow to
tell him when to strike against the Germans. His forces
went into action that summer, after the invasion of Russia.

I shall not attempt to tell the terrible tale of Yugoslavia
during the crisscross of occupation, resistance and multiple
civil wars, when peasants of different religious faiths fought
each other, when Communists fought Royalists and both
fought the Axis powers. It was a cruel conflict and, before
it ended, one-tenth of all Yugoslavs were dead.

In August, 1941, Dedijer received party orders to join a

Partisan detachment being formed near the eastern town of Kragujevac. The Communists gave him false documents and he traveled to Kragujevac in a train compartment filled with Nazi officers and from there made his way into a nearby forest, where he found a band of guerrillas. They did not yet have uniforms, but a few days later they captured four hundred when they blew up a convoy of German trucks. From these uniforms they cut the insignia and sewed red stars to their caps and collar tabs.

Even for those who have seen the most arduous conventional war, it is difficult to imagine the guerrillas' sufferings. Tito and his soldiers lived much of the time on mule meat and nettles or leaves. When winter snow was whipped up by the terrible north wind, the Bora, it bit into the ragged army. Hunger was present day and night and mass hallucinations sometimes drove the troops insane. Once an entire battalion fancied it saw in the distance a huge castle with warm smoke pouring out of the chimneys. On another occasion a brigade, imagining it smelled cooking food, rushed up to an empty field kitchen, beating battered captured mess tins.

As spring brought warmer weather, the revived units would march along singing strangely beautiful propaganda songs: "Oj Sloveni, yosh shte zhivi"—"O Slavs, you are still alive"; or "Druzhe Tito, ljubicice bela"—"Comrade Tito, O White Violet, the whole of our youth follows you"; or "Oj Chetnici [a parody of Mihailovitch's moving anthem] Italianske sluga"—"Oh Chetniks, servants of the Italians, you cannot save the Italian railways from destruction."

Often the guerrillas had to halt and tend their sick, laying out the typhus cases in tunnels filled with indescribable stench. Outside, ravenous convalescents would crawl through furrows to nibble at sprouting shoots. When a detachment entered the castled town of Jajce beside a Bosnian lake, hundreds of peasant women were discovered on all fours, licking salt beside an abandoned Nazi chemical factory.

Dedijer, who became a colonel in the Partisan forces, was wounded several times by mines and bombs. But his immense frame supported much hardship. As time went on he was assigned to Tito's own staff, where he served as a kind of chronicler of the movement, faithfully keeping a diary which has since been published in Yugoslavia under the title *Dnevnik*. In this journal he described the ghastly strife in the province of his ancestors, Bosnia-Herzegovina, in which lived many Moslems, relics of Turkish rule:

"Every night in my mother's land I saw the sky red from burning villages, whether Serb or Moslem. When we entered the little mountain town of Rogatica, which had been burned and pillaged, I had my first opportunity to see with my own eyes what Bosnian traditional hatred really meant.

"When the atrocities against the Serbs had begun, a Serbian priest was shod on his hands and knees, then saddled and ridden through the town. The Partisans and the Chetniks soon liberated Rogatica from Quisling rule, but one night the Chetniks took their revenge on the Moslems. They slaughtered every Moslem who stood taller than a rifle."

Dedijer's wife, Olga, who had borne him a daughter, Milica, in 1940, remained with her baby for a time on the outskirts of Belgrade. However, trained as a doctor, she insisted on joining the Partisans when she learned how short they were of medical aid. She left Milica in Zemun with her parents. In June, 1943, as Tito's main forces were fighting their way out of Axis encirclement near Montenegro, she was wounded in the shoulder by a bomb fragment.

One of the nurses in Olga's detachment sent for Vlado, who found her under an oak tree, blood seeping through the inadequate bandage, a great shadow already widening beneath her glowing black eyes. "Don't worry," she said quietly, "although it is a bad wound."

For ten days the Partisans fought their way northward and Olga was carried along on a thin old horse in the middle of a unit assigned to guard the casualties. On June 19, her right arm was amputated in a peasant hut while magpies in a dreary field outside picked at the summer seedlings. The surgeon wished to give her a camphor injection as a stimulant but, still conscious, she refused, saying:

"Don't waste it. Keep it for some comrade who can be saved." Ten minutes later she died.

Dedijer, who together with five other Partisans buried her on a mountainside, recalls:

"Night was falling. The wind howled and bent the huge pines. We dug her grave with our hands and knives. She lay in her white blanket, her hair almost covering her face. The wind increased. Laza, a miner comrade, a fighter from Serbia since 1941, grabbed a handful of earth. 'Vlado, we've come to the rock,' he said. The last handfuls of soil were scraped away by a comrade whom she had operated on. 'She saved my life. How we loved her.'"

Vlado, too, had been wounded in that engagement and he kept himself alive only by chewing sulfanilamide tablets parachuted by a British plane. A shell fragment was imbedded in his skull and, as the summer passed, he became partially paralyzed. Consequently when Tito's main force had escaped the German trap and reassembled to the north, he was taken out with a British liaison mission and flown to Cairo for an operation.

There, in the late autumn of 1943, I found him, heavily bandaged, with Olga's Italian pistol at his bedside as a souvenir, lying in a hospital room with another Partisan officer from whose head protruded a chunk of fleshy matter the size of a man's fist. Both recovered and Dedijer's roommate later became a Cabinet Minister—and Vlado's enemy.

I saw a good deal of Dedijer in Cairo, while he was convalescing, and he talked of the old days, of the desperate struggle and principally about three people: Olga and her tragic death; little Milica, whom he had not seen since he left Belgrade in August, 1941; and Milovan Djilas, the friend who had introduced him to Communism and who had become one of Tito's principal commanders.

This man Djilas was a hot-headed Montenegrin poet who had acquired a certain renown even before the war. Now, as a Partisan, he was famous. A British officer with Tito told me that after one battle Djilas refused to clean his bayonet, although it was caked with blood. "Leave it," he said. "Let it remind me of the Fascists I have killed."

Vlado kept referring to him, saying: "He has taught me the value of our dream. He has taught me why we must sacrifice so much. It is for what Milovan has taught me that

Olga was sacrificed. We shall make a new Yugoslavia in a new world."

When Dedijer finally recovered he was sent to Bari, in southern Italy, to help organize shipments of Allied supplies across the Adriatic to the Partisans. I saw him there early in 1944 after I had been arrested and released by the British in the village of Monopoli for trying to get to Yugoslavia. I had previously attempted to arrange to be parachuted to either Mihailovitch or Tito by the various British and American special services, but without success. Whenever one of these bickering organizations approved, the idea was vetoed by its rivals.

Near Bari, together with Dedijer, I met an unusually beautiful blonde Slovenian girl named Veronica, who had been taken by the Fascist occupiers from her home town of Ljubljana for scribbling patriotic slogans on the walls of her school and who had been imprisoned in an Italian jail.

Many years after I was to see her fascinate an Italian prince by her beauty and by her fluency in his language. "But how did you learn to speak Italian so perfectly?" he asked. "In one of your prisons," she answered.

Later she married Dedijer, bore him four children and became the stepmother of Olga's daughter, Milica.

Vlado tried unsuccessfully to help me get to Tito, who had invited me formally by letter. However, blocked by the British and American secret services, which controlled all means of entry, I didn't manage to see the Partisan leader until the early spring of 1945, in Moscow, as the war was drawing to a close.

Tito had gone there to visit Stalin, who, at the time,

greatly admired the Balkan guerrillas. It was on that occasion that I first met Dedijer's turbulent friend Djilas.

When Tito introduced me to him, Djilas said: "Ah, so you are the man who writes that our Tito is slaughtering Serbian peasants with American rifles." He turned his back. Tito patted me on the shoulder, saying: "Don't pay any attention to him."

In 1946, just after the Yugoslavs had shot down two unarmed American planes and we were on the verge of war, I drove a jeep through Yugoslavia to Greece, itself engulfed in civil strife. Djilas, then boss of propaganda and Number 2 man in the country, announced on the radio that if I entered Yugoslavia he would have me hanged as a friend of Mihailovitch, the Royalist Chetnik leader who for a time had contested Tito for control of the Yugoslav resistance. Fortunately he did not try to carry out his threat.

Later, after Tito had quarreled with Stalin, I reminded Djilas of this unfriendly promise. "Forget it," he said with a disarming smile. "Times have changed."

During that 1946 transit of Yugoslavia I stopped in Belgrade and saw Dedijer, dressed in a handsome new uniform, and his second wife, the lovely Veronica, or Vera. Vlado had been elected a member of the Communist party's Central Committee and was a prominent member of what Djilas was to dub "The New Class."

He lived in a villa in the stylish residential section, had a car and servants, played tennis with Cabinet ministers and generals and used to go on the hunts of which Tito was particularly fond. There Dedijer's poor marksmanship made him the butt of jokes.

One day some leading Communists caught a calf, clipped its hair, dyed the animal tan, tied a stag's antlers to its head and suddenly drove it from behind a bush as Vlado approached. Dedijer shot it. From then on for many weeks his telephone would ring at night and, when he answered it, there would come a loud "Mooooo."

At this time Dedijer was a bitter, arrogant man. Sometimes he would walk through the capital, see someone whose antipathy to Communism was known and ask: "What are you doing out of jail?" It was rumored that some of these persons later disappeared.

In his book *The Beloved Land*, Vlado inferentially admitted as much by writing: "My heart was bitter and hard. I met many acquaintances. I looked at everyone I met with suspicion. Was he, I wondered, the one who drank beer in Terazije Square while the corpses of the Partisans were hanging on the poles?

" 'Dear Vlado, you're alive!' a voice cried out, as an old high school friend ran up to embrace me. I glared at him.

" 'What did you do during the war?' I demanded. 'Stay at home guarding your wife?' "

Lord Acton's law on power's corrupting influence applied to these Communist friends of mine quite as perceptibly as, later on, did the Saturnic law, which was to immolate them. Dedijer, although charged with press relations and foreign diplomatic ventures, behaved with haughty conceit.

One day I asked him what his exact hierarchical position was. "I work directly under Tito," he replied. "Well then," I continued, "why do you treat the press like lepers? Tito at least behaves like a gentleman." "Didn't I ask you out for lunch?" said Vlado. A short time later he attacked me in the United Nations for spreading "imperialistic lies."

Until 1948, when the Tito-Stalin quarrel burst into the open and Yugoslavia suddenly found itself on the verge of war with all its former Communist allies, my relationships with Dedijer were curious. On the one hand, he was cold, sardonic, sometimes even hostile, and he never lost an opportunity to denounce capitalism, the West, the United States and particularly the American press. On the other hand, despite this hostility, he continued to invite me to meals and, when he was in Paris, to call upon me if only for purposes of argument.

This attitude, of course, began to change when Belgrade's foreign policy changed after the break with Moscow. All of a sudden I noticed more informality and genuine warmth in my relations with the Dedijer family. Vlado himself began to ask advice on such Western idiosyncrasies as how to hold a press conference. He wanted us to go fishing together in the mountains near Olga's grave.

Almost unconsciously and quite without restraint he became pro-American and violently anti-Soviet. He and his constant companion, Djilas, were immensely impressed when they visited the Ford factory at River Rouge; they admitted that never before had they realized how powerful a nation ours was. Vlado began to reassess his memories of the Russians. He accused them, for example, of having supported Mihailovitch against the Partisans for six whole months.

In 1949, after the Yugoslavs' quarrel with Stalin, Dedijer confided that when he attended UN meetings none of the satellite delegates spoke or nodded to him but in the lavatories they would whisper: "Bravo. Keep it up."

And he and Djilas together assured me: "You know, there is less bureaucracy in English labor unions than in our own." This was a naïve admission, for "bureaucracy" in Marxist double-talk means dictatorship.

On April 3, 1951, in Belgrade, I went with Vlado to visit Djilas. To my astonishment, Djilas talked of the need for alliance with Greece, until then still denounced by the Yugoslavs as a "Monarcho-Fascist" state. Djilas and Dedijer knew I was on the way to Athens, where I had many friends. Djilas asked me to repeat his words to the King, the Prime Minister and the Chief of the General Staff. At that time he was Tito's Number 2 and the message, he told me, could be considered as coming from the Marshal.

Djilas was wearing knickerbockers, a tweed coat, a checked shirt and no necktie. On his desk were a cap and brief case. We went for a ride in the suburbs in his chauffeur-driven American convertible and Djilas and Dedijer talked about the United States almost as if it were Yugoslavia's only faithful friend.

They said: "Our countries must work out a basis for mutual aid. In a sense we are already allies. We must negotiate with you to get American arms. And we need a common defense plan together with Greece and Turkey." These were giddy words to hear in a Communist land.

The next day, at a long country lunch, Dedijer continued: "We must now change our propaganda line. We must explain to the people that [Communist] China is really an imperialist, aggressive power." But when I asked why a mutual friend of ours, a well-known liberal Democrat, was still in jail, he replied: "It would be dangerous to release him. He would attack the government with Communist slogans."

"Do you mean," I inquired, "to imply that Dragoljub is a Communist?"

"Oh, no. But he would accuse the government of lowering living standards and increasing the hardships of the peasant."

"Yet that is true, isn't it?" I remarked. Dedijer regarded me with puzzlement.

I wrote in my diary: "Vlado is obviously confused by Belgrade's dispute with Moscow. He is groping toward Western democracy like so many Yugoslavs. England with its [then] Socialism seems to be a convenient stepping stone and Nye Bevan a guide."

In 1951 Dedijer was engaged in writing an authorized biography of Marshal Tito, a book that was to become a best seller and earn its author approximately half a million dollars. The idea, in fact, had originally been mine.

But what I had proposed to Tito was that he should write his own autobiography, using Vlado as a kind of Marxist ghost. The ghost, in this case, took over and finally sold the venture to *Life* magazine. My hope had been to get first rights for *The New York Times* if Tito wrote his own story.

Vlado at that period saw the Marshal every day. He told me they had recently gone for a drive together, Tito at the wheel. "For God's sake, be careful," Dedijer pleaded with Yugoslavia's head man as they skidded around a corner. "I have five children and I don't know what they'd do without me." Tito laughed and said: "Don't worry. I used to be a test driver for Mercedes Benz in 1910."

It was essentially because of this intimacy with Tito that Dedijer felt confusion perhaps but no great inner wrench when he suddenly found himself considering Russia as a hostile land instead of Communism's perfect dream. For, when the dispute with Moscow came, neither Tito nor his lieutenants considered this a break with Communism as such.

Tito's essential complaint, indeed, was that Stalin, by deifying himself and tyrannizing his country, had abandoned the true Marxist-Leninist creed. He contended that he, Tito, not Stalin, was the true practicant.

This is important to remember. Although he broke with Russia and the other satellites, although he engaged in cold war with China, although he allied himself with Greece and Turkey, both members of NATO, and accepted American aid, even when his quarrel with the Kremlin was at its most acrid point Tito held himself to be a faithful Communist.

The ultimate paradox, however, was that once rebelliously independent thoughts were nurtured in the ranks of Titoism, this freedom carried on to even more heretical conclusions. A heresy developed within the Titoist heresy itself. And Djilas and Dedijer, those two veterans of Yugoslav Communism, became the symbols of this revolt inside a revolt.

The result of Djilas' deliberations after the break with Stalin and after his own extensive travels in the West was a series of articles in the official organ of Yugoslav Communism, *Borba*, during late 1953 and early 1954. At first these occasioned but mild interest. Djilas did not experience real trouble until he criticized the "caste system" that had arisen in the ruling hierarchy and the growth of a privileged Communist "aristocracy." Later he ferociously expounded this idea in his well-known book *The New Class*.

The *Borba* articles proclaimed the following theory: Yugoslavia's class struggle had ended, therefore the enemy was no longer capitalism but party bureaucracy; bureaucrats were blocking progress by preventing freedom of expression; as a consequence, all forms of despotism, Stalinist, Leninist or under any other label, must be abandoned. This credo, of course, was itself as dangerous to Titoism as Titoism was to Stalinism.

Djilas reasoned that Communism would come about spontaneously, not by being imposed, because it "is not the product of geniuses or of noble wishes and purposes but of social necessity."

He concluded: "The possibility of two Socialist parties emerging in our country cannot be discounted. . . . The Leninist type of both party and state (dictatorship by means of the party) has become and must become obsolete everywhere and always. . . . The party is depressed and without an ideology. Its dogma was taken from it through the democratization trend and nothing has replaced it. . . . The name Communism is good but it has been compromised. It is a synonym for totalitarianism in this country as well as Russia."

Imagine advocacy of a two-party system by the head of

a monolithic propaganda apparatus within a monolithic
Communist state; and also imagine this being endorsed in
the party's official journal by that same man, Number 2 in
the dictatorial hierarchy, the man who had worshiped Tito
and almost died for him, the man who as a youth had suffered prison and torture for conspiratorial Communism, the
man of the bayonet caked with blood, the man who had
even sat at Stalin's feet (when I met him in Moscow in
1945), declaiming Montenegrin poems.

The resulting storm was immense and it became greater
when Djilas committed the unpardonable sin. Not only did
he refuse to recant; he resigned from the party. He developed his ideas even further in that later treatise *The New
Class.*

The case brought misery to Dedijer. When it exploded
in the Communist Central Committee, Vlado was the only
member to stick by Djilas, his oldest living party friend. He
admitted that perhaps the renegade had been excessive in
some of his arguments and wrong in some of his conclusions but he defended his right to dissent. "Each of us has
a right to think for himself," said Dedijer. "I am no robot."

This statement was heard in hostile silence and, when he
had finished, Dedijer was dismissed from the party. He was
deprived of all official positions and ousted from his villa.
His mother, one of the most prominent women in the new
regime, tore up her party card. And Steve, his brother, the
Princeton graduate who had served with the American
Army as a paratrooper, was discharged from his post as head
of the Yugoslav Atomic Energy Commission. Steve's wife

was persuaded by social and economic pressure to divorce him.

On January 17, 1954, Djilas was expelled from the Communist Politburo and Central Committee, despite Dedijer's defense. Later that year both he and Dedijer gave forthright interviews to foreign correspondents in which they spoke out against what they termed "errors" in Yugoslav political life.

On January 24, 1955, the two friends were tried jointly for having uttered "slanderous statements to the correspondents of the foreign press" who "wrongly interpreted the situation in the country." The press was barred from the trial. Dedijer, oddly enough, was defended by a well-known Croatian attorney named Ivo Politeo, who had defended Tito in 1928 when the Communist leader was sentenced to five years' hard labor by a Royalist court.

Djilas and Dedijer were convicted, given suspended sentences and allowed to return home. But they were placed on probation and refused all work. On November 10, 1956, Djilas was again arrested. He had just published a critical article in a Western journal and was charged with violating his probation. As a result he was sent to prison. While he was there, two of his manuscripts, smuggled out of the country, were published abroad. And Dedijer was placed in almost equally effective cold storage, being wholly ostracized by Yugoslavia's monolithic society.

The Saturnic law in Yugoslavia operated, on the whole, in far milder fashion than is its usual implacable custom. When the revolution devoured Dedijer it did not slay him;

instead it sought to starve him into submission. He was refused all jobs for which he applied, including a chair as
professor at Belgrade University. And, for a long time, he
was refused a passport to travel, although he had been offered a position in Manchester University, England.

Furthermore, all his former friends and party colleagues
were ordered to ostracize him. The evident hope was that,
driven to isolation and despair, seeing his family suffer the
consequences of his independent stand, he would in the
end knuckle under.

Dedijer had earned a substantial fortune from foreign
royalties on his book *Tito*, published in 1953. Nevertheless,
as a good Communist and as a loyal husband who, despite
his second marriage, still cherished Olga's memory, he had
turned this entire sum over to the state with the request
that it be used to build a hospital named for his first wife.
As a result, when disgrace engulfed him and his family, they
found themselves penniless. He and Steve turned to writing
nonpolitical articles and book reviews for foreign maga-
zines, most of which were left-wing liberal or Socialist and
therefore in no position to pay large fees. The family sub-
sisted meagerly.

Not long after Djilas and Dedijer first fell from power,
I had one of my many talks with Tito. He was staying at
his villa on the Slovenian lake of Bled, where he pursued a
favorite hobby, hunting the auerhahn or capercaillie, a
turkey-sized grouse which is somewhat gruesomely stalked
only during the mating season. After an extensive and ram-
bling conversation on world questions, I asked the Marshal
about the two renegades, his former friends.

Tito turned quite purple. For a moment, he only sputtered, walking up and down, peering through the window at the rain-swept lake. Then he said: "As for Djilas, we have forgotten him already. He had no real influence, no popular backing. He voluntarily quit the party and we will never, never permit him to rejoin.

"However, Dedijer's is a different case. We hold nothing serious against him even though the masses may find it difficult to understand why he supported Djilas. Time will iron out his position. His health is bad and we will do our best to see he gets some rest."

Just what kind of a "rest" this was I discovered the next time I went to Belgrade. I visited Vlado in his humble new apartment, where the entire family lived jammed together. He was astonishingly modest and obviously disconsolate. I noted at the time:

"Poor fellow, he is down on his uppers. His back is troubling him; war wounds. The doctors now say that two vertebrae are smashed and must be fused together. He fears an operation because the odds in favor of success aren't good. And he doesn't know what will become of his family if he dies. He walks with a stoop and haltingly.

"He has no source of income although he hopes to continue writing for foreign publications. Apart from those book royalties he gave the government before his troubles, he had saved some money to erect a small monument on Olga's grave. Fortunately, he says, work on this has not yet been started and he can now exist for a while on the funds.

"He lives very simply and says: 'Thank goodness I never got used to such things as iceboxes.' He and his family eat mainly beans and bread. Now that he is so hard up, he confesses to a realization of how the poor must be suffering from steadily rising prices in the inflated Yugoslav economy.

"For a year the party tried to force Vera to divorce him. She refused and so they ousted her. He himself did not resign but was expelled. The party also tried to induce his mother (who has had a stroke) to denounce him. But she exploded in a rage and quit.

"Vlado's five children [four by Vera, and Milica, Olga's girl] have all had virus pneumonia and are greatly weakened by it. His mother and he hope to go to the Dalmatian coast soon to live in a peasant house and restore the youngsters' health."

It was odd sitting in the study of this old revolutionary, looking at his bookshelves—lined with volumes on Tito and the Partisans. He said sadly that almost all his friends had deserted him. He wrote Tito to complain of what was happening to him and his family but never received an answer. He pretended to think Tito never got the letter, but this was deliberate self-deception.

Indeed, it was curious to see how his admiration for Tito seemed to continue despite everything. He spoke of him as the "first real Yugoslav." He was absolutely positive Tito would never rejoin the Russian fold. "But after Tito, what?" he asked aloud, shrugging his shoulders. Then he continued: "Until 1948 Stalin was my god. Now I have no more gods—nor will I ever have another."

In our age we have seen many people who have left one dominating dogma only to seek another for support. Many a former Communist has found refuge in the arms of the Roman Catholic Church. But for Dedijer, when he discovered himself deserted and oppressed by the revolution he had blindly and even ruthlessly supported, there was no search for another crutch to shore him up in his despair. For the first time, he realized, he had nothing but himself, his own feet and his own soul to rely on.

Dedijer insisted he had remained true to Djilas not so much because he agreed with all his ideas—"Djilas went much too far"—but because he was a friend and: "I am a Serb, and I have been taught to stand by my friends." Then he added these oddly non-Marxist thoughts: "I have my ethics, Christian ethics. Europe and its Christian civilization is one thing and Yugoslavia is with Europe. Soviet Russia is another thing. And it is not European."

Vlado talked about the old days when he was rising in the hierarchy; of how Tito had offered him the ambassadorship to China in 1949. He talked of our prewar meetings, of dead friends, and of Olga. He recalled his plans for the sanatorium in Olga's name. Whenever he wrote to inquire about this, he received no answer.

He was then working on a doctoral thesis on international law with which he hoped at last to persuade the local university to give him a professorship. In the meantime, he had no job nor any regular source of income. But he said proudly: "My conscience is clean and I am calm."

He was most philosophical, contending: "I do not hate anyone. I have contempt for my friends who have deserted me. But I see that everything is not black and white. There are many grays in the picture. But poor Djilas. He is a

Montenegrin. He is by heritage a rough and violent man and now he hates everyone with violence. For him all is black or white. I always told him that he went too far. Yet such is his temperament, a moody mountain man."

Vlado learned a much deeper understanding for the Yugoslav people and their problems. He said: "Today I know them better and I know how much they suffer. Wherever I go, to my amazement there is always some stranger who greets me warmly. Quite recently Milica, who is fifteen, needed a new dress. She hadn't had one in two years and she looked pathetic because she has grown so much. The other girls in school began to tease her and she was miserable. So Vera took her to a dressmaker. But the dressmaker refused to accept payment, saying: 'We know you have no income and no pension.' "

On several occasions tears came into his eyes. Quite clearly the most terrible blow for him was expulsion from the Communist party, the church that had excommunicated him. He explained that he had not joined in a light-hearted mood and this total ban shook him to the heart. He was also deeply hurt by the cold-shoulder treatment of his friends.

He pointed with deep sentiment to a picture of himself and Djilas looking down at the tomb of Karl Marx in London. This was one of the few photographs on the wall of a rather shabby room, filled with the stale air of overcrowding. Time and again he remarked on how fortunate it was that he had never become accustomed too long to a really luxurious life. "For that I can thank my stars. I am ready for what lies ahead when there is no more money."

In 1956, when I was visiting Belgrade to see Tito, I took Vlado and Vera out for dinner in an old Serbian restaurant called Dva Jelena, the Two Stags. At the neighboring table, with his family, was the judge who had tried Dedijer for his "heresies." They looked right through each other.

Vlado had taken treatment for his back and seemed more confident about his health. And Vera, although she did not yet have a passport, was learning English because she had been invited to England to visit Jenny Lee, the wife of Aneurin (Nye) Bevan, the fiery Socialist leader.

Dedijer told me he had at last received positive information that the authorities had taken down Olga's picture and name from the modest memorial he had erected in her honor. He wrote to Ranković, Minister of Interior and chief of the secret police, complaining about this; again, no reply.

His finances were still barely holding out, largely because his Rome publisher sent him the royalties for an Italian edition of his Tito book, about which he had forgotten. He figured he could live without starving for six more months.

Again and again he had applied for his doctoral examination at Belgrade University in order to become a professor. But the university authorities kept putting off any action. Now he was writing more. He had begun work on a novel about a man in love with two women—one dead and one alive, himself and Olga and Vera. He confided, to my own and Vera's embarrassment: "I don't know which is the stronger force."

It was strange to regard the life of this outcast, once so arrogant, once so optimistic. As a pariah of the regime he had helped to install he used conspiratorial techniques learned in the Communist underground. His house was watched and his telephone was tapped by the police. To test censorship, he wrote frequent letters to himself under various false signatures. So far they had all arrived.

Vlado, his five children, wife and mother were then living on about $60 a month. They would order about ten ounces of meat three times a week; for the rest, bread, soup, cabbage. They had learned to do without most amusements like the movies. Vlado forwent his favorite soccer games in a vast stadium he himself had ordered built when he was in the government. But he and Vera still attended concerts, where he insisted on the extravagance of sitting in the same seats they used to occupy prior to his disgrace.

"When one dies, one must die as an aristocrat," he said —an unusual comment from a Communist. "There is no point dying like a beggar when you used to be at the top."

Vlado said a few people, a very few, still spoke to him, so he had worked out a formula to test the courage of erstwhile associates. On the streets he would greet anyone who used to hold higher rank than he himself; but he expected those formerly below him in the hierarchy to greet him first. He would nod once to the men who had outranked him and, if they did not acknowledge his nod, the next time he cut them. He would nod three times to women of his acquaintance and then ignore them if they did not acknowledge his greeting.

As an outcast Dedijer found he had to concentrate on day-to-day problems. "If you start thinking about what is going to happen tomorrow, then you are finished," he confided. "I cannot think of the future. It only brings worries."

Boro, his eldest son, disapproved of this quarrel with the regime. He admonished his father: "You shouldn't do this. I was obliged to fight for you in school and I don't like to fight." But Milica, a strikingly pretty girl, was being courted by the sons of two Cabinet Ministers.

In this cruelly isolated life Dedijer gradually evolved a new personal ideology which he continued to label "Communism," just as Tito, when he broke with Stalin, proclaimed that he was a better Communist than the Soviet boss. But Vlado's Communism was becoming as different from Tito's as Tito's was from Stalin's. Thus, he assured me:

"There is no real Socialism in the world today. In fact, I think the nearest thing to Communism can be found in the kibbutzim of Israel, according to what I hear about them. If war comes in the Middle East I intend to volunteer in the Israeli Army and to get out of here some way or other in order to go and fight with them."

Nevertheless, he continued, "I stick to our 1952 party constitution which says that any party member is free to criticize. The Communist party should be proud of me. Certainly I don't want to join any other ideology. I am just out of one Catholic Church and I don't want to get into another. I suppose, ideologically speaking, I want to be a freelance."

He commented sarcastically about the Russians, whom he now increasingly despised: "For thirty years Khrushchev licked Stalin's boots; yet today he denigrates him. That explains better than anything else the kind of thing that is also going on here.

"But my life is an open book. I don't try to hide my feelings. I look upon things objectively. I don't want to make any more trouble for my family. After all, I am not an inhuman father. Furthermore, I don't really hate anyone although I have contempt for many. I am the historian of our revolution, and as a historian I must remain objective.

"I never learned Marx from textbooks. I learned from practice, from our revolution. Everything you take only from dogma is bad. It must be balanced against the good learned from practice. That is Titoism. And I am applying Titoism to Titoism. This philosophy has saved me. I claim that ethics cannot be destroyed. Every society has its ethics and they are constant in European society. They are, of course, not constant in Russia because Russia isn't truly part of Europe."

Dedijer insisted that Karl Marx was useful in analyzing only the first stages of Socialism and capitalism. Today, he argued, "there is no pure system of either capitalism or Socialism; there are only elements of both: the new order and the old order, all mixed up together."

To this he appended the observation that in 1953, when he was in the United States with Kardelj, another Yugoslav boss, Kardelj told him: "There is more Socialism in the United States than in the Soviet Union."

With Serbian egotism Vlado said: "I am the last Mohican. I am sticking to our party regulations laid down in

1952, even if our party expelled me. The others have re-
treated. They are all crazy.

"From my own case I learned the need for tolerance and
now I am learning tolerance for everyone. Perhaps this is
the result of my early Christian education. I fought, starved
and died with these people, these Yugoslavs of mine. I cannot be proclaimed an enemy. Nor can I recant.

"This has been an excellent moral experience for me. I
see how lazy and arrogant I once was. I did not even know
the price of bread. When I went to ride in a bus for the
first time after my downfall, I entered by the wrong door.
I found my bureaucratic life had been quite different from
that of the ordinary man. This has been a marvelous and
true lesson.

"The last time I had ever studied Socialism was in high
school. Then the revolution came along and swept me into
its embrace. Now, for the first time, I have plenty of time
to learn. It is a good experience for me and it is wonderful
for my children.

"They were little bureaucrats before. Branko used to go
to the door and shout: 'Where is the car?' Now they know
the value of money. Now they take part in our family coun-
cil discussing accounts. I am the finance minister. I cannot
go to soccer games any more. I, too, must make my sac-
rifices for our community. But, nevertheless, I am much
criticized as a finance minister.

"I have had to put my children on a different spending
level; no more luxuries. I cannot even buy books. But I
still insist on concerts. Vera and I need music. Above all,

we love Schumann, Schubert and Mendelssohn. The German romantic composers were a reaction to the political sterility of Napoleon. I suppose that is why we love them so much.

"But don't feel sorry for me. I have learned much. And remember this, Cy: Whatever occurs, I am not going to eat dirt. If you have to eat dirt once in your life you will have to say it is good forever."

One day on another trip to Belgrade, I ate a modest lunch in the Dedijer apartment and then went for a walk with Vera and Vlado in the Kalemegdan Park, an ancient Turkish fortification overlooking the confluence of the Danube and Sava rivers. As we were strolling under the battlements, Vlado said to me:

"I hope you don't mind walking, but there is something I wished to tell you and, despite all the precautions I try to take, I can never know for certain if my house is bugged or not. I didn't want to take a chance."

He then recounted a curious incident. Some weeks previously he and his mother were staying with the children in a peasant hut on the Dalmatian Coast and one night they were awakened by the sound of shooting. When Vlado rushed to the door and flung it open, a man in the uniform of captain of the U.D.B.A. (Secret Police) staggered in and almost immediately died. Who was he? Why was he shot? What was he doing outside Dedijer's abode? Was he spying on the family and shot by mistake for Vlado in the darkness?

"This is a strange life," said Dedijer. "I conspired in our underground for the sake of the people, to improve their happiness. I fought in our Partisan Army for the sake of the same people. I helped to bring in this regime for the sake of the people. And now what have I accomplished?"

He told me the latest sardonic joke whispered about Yugoslavia. A priest in Catholic Croatia remonstrated with a peasant who was no longer attending mass. After the peasant had missed several services, the priest called upon him and noticed four pictures clustered in the traditional ikon corner.

"Who are they?" asked the priest, observing in fact that they were Stalin, Eisenhower, Lollobrigida and Tito.

"But these are my ikons," said the peasant.

"Do you pray to them?"

"Of course, Father," said the peasant.

"To the first I say: 'My Father which art in heaven.' To the second I say: 'Give us each day our daily bread.' To the third I say: 'Lead us not into temptation.' And to the fourth I say: 'Forgive us our trespasses as we forgive those who trespass against us.' "

When we were walking home, Dedijer said to me that while he was facing trial Tito had been visiting India and Nehru had intervened on his behalf. Vlado had heard rumors he was about to be given twelve years in prison; he believed Nehru's intervention persuaded Tito to order only a suspended sentence.

To my astonishment, in 1957 Dedijer was permitted to leave Belgrade to give some lectures to Scandinavian Socialists. His family were not issued passports as insurance against his return, but it was evident his situation had improved.

On the way back from Stockholm Vlado stayed with me in Paris. He reported that Yugoslavia was still seething with disappointment and anger as a result of the previous autumn's Hungarian uprising and the brutal Russian repression of it.

"We Serbs," he said, "are after all much the same as the Hungarians, much as we may hate them for all the wars we've had over the centuries. Give either of our peoples a couple of good slogans and we will fight anyone."

He believed Tito had failed to help the Hungarians, despite his disapproval of Moscow's methods, because he feared a successful revolt in Budapest might have spread into Yugoslavia. This, in turn, would either have threatened to overthrow the entrenched, privileged class now running Yugoslavia or have doomed it to new subservience to Russia in turn for help in quelling an upheaval.

Tito, he concluded, was wise from a selfish, personal point of view because he understood the violence inherent in the Serbs. "Nevertheless," said Vlado, "it is wonderful to be a Serb—despite the trials we bring upon ourselves." As a consequence of his Scandinavian talks, Vlado had heard, he was again in trouble for "behaving in a hostile way." This puzzled him because he thought he had been exceptionally discreet. Notwithstanding, he said: "Let's eat well today. When I get back I guess I'll be going to prison and my diet will be nothing but beans."

Dedijer's new difficulties with Tito's regime had, in fact, arisen from one particular lecture in Stockholm. What did he say that enraged Belgrade?

He said that the gap between the highest and lowest salaries in the U.S.S.R. is bigger than in many capitalist countries. Employees of the coercive apparatus have especially high salaries.

He said that a superstate has been created in the U.S.S.R. with a total monopoly in society. A specific form of totalitarian state capitalism has been created in which the exploitation of man by man is the fact of life.

He observed that in Soviet society the ethical and moral principles are neglected and the emphasis is on coercion and the threat of coercion. Every movement which puts aside ethics is sowing the seeds of its own destruction.

He said that in the Soviet Union there exists a physical barrier between the people and the leaders, a special psychology, a psychology of bureaucracy whose main characteristics is intolerance.

He observed in Moscow's foreign policy "a tendency toward expansion and hegemony." He declared: "Democracy cannot be taken in small doses; it either exists or it does not exist."

In his official biography of Tito, Dedijer had defined Socialism as a society "in which there will be no exploitation of man by man, in which an individual will be freed of the fetters of the state."

He insisted he still believed this but added that in Russia the bureaucracy, which ran things under Stalin, had been replaced under Khrushchev by a technocracy in which the "army increasingly played a role similar to that of the former Junkers in Prussia."

He pointed out that for two decades Khrushchev and his colleagues had helped Stalin commit "some of the most atrocious crimes in history" and had thereby lost for themselves "any human integrity." But the struggle inside the Soviet leadership, he said, is not over. "Whoever gets control of the army no doubt will be the victor."

He spoke of the Hungarian uprising and Russia's savage repression of it.

He said, that using brute power, the U.S.S.R. was attempting to force the belief that Soviet forms of development and Soviet views were the only ones valid. The Hungarian way to Socialism would have been expressed in a coalition of liberal forces. But in Hungary Russian imperialism has bared itself to the skin."

He drew a most interesting comparison between Soviet and American methods. He informed the Swedes that when France torpedoed E.D.C. [the European Defense Community project] at a very critical phase of the Cold War, American tanks never surrounded Paris and fired on it, nor was [Premier] Mendès-France proclaimed a traitor and taken as a captive to unknown whereabouts, let us say Portugal.

And he concluded by saying that evidently, in the U.S.S.R. there were as yet no signs of any desire to change fundamentally the policies of the time of Stalin.

These were peculiar words from a man who claimed that in his own way he was still a Communist. No wonder Belgrade was angry, for much of the criticism aimed at Russia could be applied with equal force to Yugoslavia.

And, oddly enough, just as the Titoist administration again seemed prepared to lower the boom on him, Dedijer was accused by American propagandists of spreading Yugoslav propaganda. The unofficial American organization Radio Free Europe sent out a strangely foolish "background guidance memorandum" to its various offices. This asserted that Tito had sent Dedijer abroad to arrange co-operation with Western Socialists and that there was no genuine difference between the two men.

Fortunately, on his return, Vlado escaped further punishment and his financial position was improved by the combination of lecture fees and new contracts he had arranged for book reviews and articles.

In February, 1958, when I was again in Belgrade on a trip, I telephoned Vlado, who said: "You are a good Serb so come over and have Serbian beans." Despite the fact that he had managed to stay out of jail things were going drearily.

His son Boro, now thirteen, was in the hospital. Two of the other children were with relatives in Slovenia recovering from illnesses. Vera was suffering from colitis and an infected liver and his mother had diabetes and all her remaining teeth had been extracted. She was so sensitive about her complete toothlessness that she refused to come out and say hello. "Wait till she gets her new false set," said Vlado.

After lunch, he showed me a weekly schedule he had prepared for himself. On every day's agenda was carefully written out the time to rise, the time to have breakfast, what to do each hour, which books to read, how many minutes of exercise.

Although he was still banned from any public job he was able to read continually in the public library and at the university. He was teaching himself German. He kept on writing book reviews and learned articles for foreign publications. He would give himself schoolteacher grades on these efforts—A, B, C: good, fair, passing.

He told me that so far as he knew all checks sent to him in payment for articles were received by the State Bank, which made no trouble about converting them into Yugoslav dinars. But his isolation continued. A former Yugoslav Ambassador, then assigned to the Foreign Ministry, had ventured to speak to him in the street one day and was quickly put on probation by the Communist party.

Dedijer gave me bad news of Djilas. His prison diet was inadequate and he was suffering from the lack of heat. "But Djido [Djilas' nickname] is fearless," Dedijer said. "Don't forget, most of his male ancestors were killed in violent ways for similarly independent views. Djido won't recant. I'm frightened for him. When he was in prison before the war he once tried to commit suicide with a knife. I hope he doesn't break this time. They're trying to drive him in that direction."

Vlado and Vera were in a mood of grave discouragement. When Vera discovered how ill she was, she and Vlado sat one day talking to each other, forgetting that their little girl, Bojana, was in the next room and could overhear. Vlado said: "If you get worse, I guess there will be nothing to do but take poison, all of us."

Bojana rushed out and told the other children: "We are all going to take poison in our bread and die."

Boro complained: "That hurts your belly. It's better to jump out of the window."

Their mother had to explain it was just a joke. She said to me: "It's so hard to watch yourself, to watch yourself all the time."

Several times each month Dedijer used to call on the parents of his first wife, Olga. The poor old people had absolutely nothing to do. They lived together in one room of their former apartment, talking of the past. Despite his love for them, Vlado grew terribly bored. He made a practice of keeping a deck of cards there and would play a game of solitaire while talking with them. He had invented a complicated scoring system to produce the illusion of competing against himself and preserved a running score for months on end.

He told me Steve, his brother, was living in Zagreb and having a difficult time. A friend of Steve's had recently been summoned by the police and told that Steve was about to be arrested. Vlado didn't know if this was true or if the authorities were merely spreading menacing tales in order to scare away his few remaining friends.

Some days later I took Vlado and Vera back to our favorite restaurant, Dva Jelena, where we sat in an obscure corner. Dedijer confided that the son of one of Tito's principal lieutenants, a man we both knew well, was getting his father into trouble.

A couple of years ago in school the students had been instructed to write an essay. The boy's theme was as follows: "In Yugoslavia there are two classes. There is the governing class to which my father and his associates and I belong. And then there is the working class." The teacher was furious and wanted to expel him.

187

Later on the youngster spent several months in Paris staying with the Yugoslav Ambassador. He used to hang around with Left Bank intellectuals and refused to go home at the end of his holiday. To everybody's embarrassment his mother had to be sent to France to bring him back against his will.

Dedijer informed me that he had been visited by two English Labour party M.P.'s who had heard that Djilas was suffering from the cold in his prison cell. He told the Englishmen: "When you people win the next elections the first thing you had better do is put radiators in your jails. You may need them later."

In the summer of 1959 I again saw Dedijer and noted of our conversations: "Contrary to what I had imagined, he still seems to be surviving relatively well. His mother now proudly displays her new false teeth. Two of the kids are away with relatives. The others seem happy. Boro, the one with rheumatic fever, has improved. Milica, now eighteen, is studying architecture at the university.

"Vlado said he is making almost $100 a month and they can live on that without trouble. He keeps writing for foreign Socialist papers on non-Yugoslav subjects. I read a huge batch of stuff he showed me from Indian, English and German publications.

"He has again been invited to accept a one-year fellowship at Manchester University in England and in October he will apply once more for his passport. Each time he has tried before and been refused he has been forced by Yugoslav regulations to wait six months before another application. He seems optimistic, however.

"There is a new amnesty statute, permitting the freeing of prisoners, if the regime so desires, after they have served one-third of their sentence. Djilas is eligible. I asked Vlado if he thought Djilas might be freed. He was skeptical. Djilas' wife still sees him fairly regularly and says he insists on being treated exactly the same way as other prisoners. His rheumatism is worse.

"He is reading and writing all the time, now working on Njegoš, the most famous Montenegrin poet. He told his wife he wants to turn over all his royalties on *The New Class*, his widely read book, published abroad, to some foreign Socialist enterprise. But Mrs. Djilas doesn't like the thought. She has just been permitted to receive about $4,000 royalties on his second book, *Land Without Justice*, so that she and their child are rather well off."

Vlado had been questioned by the U.D.B.A. again but had experienced no further inconvenience. Some of his friends were also taken in for questioning; yet nobody was arrested. Little by little things seemed to be easing up. But he was worried about an *agent provocateur* who sought to visit him in order to stir up trouble. He was positive this man worked for the secret police.

I wrote to Dedijer after my departure. He told me later that my letter had been a good omen. Vera and Boro received passports and went to Vienna to a hospital where he could be treated. The Austrian Socialist party invited them so Vlado didn't have to worry about expense.

Boro's illness was very strange; his nerves were affected. Vlado said: "I hope that the doctors in Vienna, the best in Europe for children, will find out what it is. Boro is a nice boy, although born under the strains of war years. Also, all that has happened since 1954 has affected him in a serious way.

"Children can worry and suffer more than grownups and you never know it. Milica is studying architecture. She is a very good girl. She works every evening until midnight. We go to the concerts often and I take long walks in the night around the streets where I spent my childhood. Belgrade is very lovely in the dark."

Later I received this message in Paris: "If a copy of Pasternak's book is hanging around your office please do send it to me. I have already received three copies from friends abroad and all three were stolen by people who are close to me. Olga's mother keeps asking if I can find a copy for her. There is a great demand for that book here."

How pitiful, this hunger for the Russian poet's novel, *Dr. Zhivago. Zhivago*, in all Slavonic tongues, derives from the root word *life*. And whether in the Dedijers' shabby, dank flat or in the drab outside world of the Belgrade that was "free," the craving was for life, for air, for that spark of freedom and originality treasured by Boris Pasternak himself through all his years of disappointment, that spark which was to disgrace him, punish his friends, yet earn him the ardent admiration of millions of Communism's demi-slaves. I sent Vlado two more copies of the book. I don't know where they ended up.

Some time afterward I received ghastly news about Branko, Vlado's second son. To understand what happened it is necessary to understand Vlado himself, his people, the land he lived in, and all that stubborn pride even little Branko had inherited.

I wonder if in this long account, pieced together from the odd notes and memories of almost a quarter century, I have been able to give a sufficiently vivid picture of Vlado, a rebel within a rebellion that itself rebelled against the matrix of world Communism.

Consider the individual: huge, egotistical, athletic, with a fine brain and education; he came of good bourgeois stock but discarded this heritage for the sake of the revolution of his dreams. His grandfather had been a Cabinet Minister in the old royal government. His mother was once lady-in-waiting to the Queen.

He himself never discarded a curious kind of snobbery. In his old orthodox-Communist days he often dropped the names of Stalin or Tito extraneously into conversation. Later, these were replaced by the names of Nye Bevan, his close English friend, whom he visited during the latter's last fatal illness, and of Mrs. Roosevelt, whom he had come to know when he was a UN delegate for Tito.

He fought through a civil war and Partisan campaign so incredibly bloody that no one can quite imagine its brutalizing effect on those who managed to survive. Nor can one imagine what those Yugoslavs did to each other: Royalist Chetnik to Communist Partisan, Partisan to pro-Hitler Croatian Ustasha; Serb to Croat, Croat to Bosnian, Macedonian to Serb; Roman Catholic to Orthodox, Orthodox to Moslem, and vice versa. I still have photographs of Chetniks happily cutting the throat of a pinioned Partisan, pictures of Serbs holding baskets filled with Croat eyes, and, again, vice versa. No one can comprehend the gouging, the stabbing, the burning, the raping, the hanging, the torture, Slav against German and Italian, Slav against Slav, all done in the name of a creed, an ideology, an imperial obsession or a nationalistic dream.

By nature the South Slavs are given to destruction and boasting. In 1937 a Yugoslav friend of mine entered the United States as a diplomat. He was met in New York by a colleague and taken to see the sights. From the top of the Empire State Building he looked down on the magnificent panorama, then turned and said: "Ah, how wonderful it would feel to blow this up."

That same man, two years later, greeted me at his native town of Split when I arrived on a little freight boat loaded with hissing turkeys, on the morning of a national election day. The bodies of three people slain during political arguments were being removed from the waterfront. When I remarked on this, he turned to me with pride and commented: "But surely you must know more Yugoslavs are killed in an election than Greeks in any Greek revolution."

I have seen a fourteen-year-old boy in Sarajevo fighting a grown man with a knife. And, in that same lovely city, still dotted with minarets, I have seen a friendly debate in a café turn into a devastating riot. Every man present joined in with fists, knives, chairs and bottles while the police waited carefully outside, unwilling to spoil the fun. This was a country which suffered 1,400,000 dead during World War II. But, of that huge figure, nearly 10 per cent of the total population, most of them killed one another.

It was the Communists, in the end, with their brilliant

organization and fierce resolve, who emerged victorious from the holocaust. And high in the ranks of those Communists was Colonel Vladimir Dedijer, ruthless, vain and confident in his position as the intimate of Tito and the best friend of Tito's chief ideological lieutenant, the hot-tempered Milovan Djilas.

It was Dedijer who worshiped Stalin, who revered Tito, who had contempt for those who disagreed with him, who neither cared nor wished to imagine the hardships of the bulk of his fellow countrymen, who happily distributed false statistics and wrongly-based reports on his nation's welfare, who regarded the press (his old profession) as something to be bullied into an ideological harness.

Yet, deep within him, the glow of humanity continued to burn warmly. Friendship proved more powerful than dogma, and loyalty to another human being was to develop into loyalty to all mankind. Disgrace was a blessing he came to welcome and travail cleaned away the dross of self-deception.

He still believed himself a Communist as he was gnawed by the Revolution's cruel Saturnic law. But, if this was Communism, it was the kind of Communism dreamed of by the early French and German Marxists, compounded of freedom, social democracy, individual rights and egalitarianism, built upon a Socratic ethic.

Dedijer was a man neither afraid to fight nor, in the end, ashamed to admit where he had been wrong before, ready to start life again upon a more humble plane. This soldier who had thought little of killing and less of being killed developed a strange gentleness in adversity.

He continued to reminisce about the aspirations of a revolutionary past while attacking the sins of a revolutionary present, never entirely distinguishing between them. He changed the very essence of his thoughts without daring to alter their ideological label. In the end, eviscerated by the revolution, talking of administering poison to himself, his obstinate old mother and the children if Vera should sicken and die, he still refused to die, this Resistentialist.

He lived the threadbare, penurious life of a scholar, refusing to "eat dirt," as he said, because one could never again lose its taste. His wife suffered silently and watched her children, deprived of the privileges that once had been their heritage, cut off and isolated from their fellows.

One result of this was that little Branko, a tough and fearless lad, got mixed up when he was twelve years old with a gang of youngsters engaged in minor mischief. They smashed windows and snatched hubcaps from Belgrade's relatively few cars.

As I learned much later, a secret police agent, noticing this, took Branko aside and threatened him. He said that to avoid serious trouble he must report to the U.D.B.A. on everyone his parents saw. In other words, he was to become the Revolution's spy. Branko refused, but he was desperately worried and his parents couldn't find out why.

Then Branko was held up before his class in school as a disgrace. When he failed an examination his teacher called him to the front of the room and publicly lectured him as a miserable example of "anti-regime elements." The

U.D.B.A. again approached him with warnings. Yet all this remained Branko's private secret, the inner torture of a very harassed boy who felt within himself the injustices slowly throttling his father.

Late in 1959 I was traveling in the Antipodes. In New Zealand, where I had stopped off after visiting Antarctica, I received a batch of mail forwarded to me by my office. This contained a letter sent by Steve Dedijer from Belgrade dated September 10, who told me that Vlado's 13-year-old son Branko failed in an exam and committed suicide.

With this was enclosed a Serbian notice, published in the local press, announcing the death on September 7 of "Our Dear Branko Dedijer."

Only months afterward was I able to find out the dismal details of this tragedy. Branko had taken his examination again, without success. He had come home one afternoon when the other children were playing elsewhere and his parents and grandmother were out. From a closet he took his father's leather belt. Then he went into the back yard and hanged himself from a tree.

When Vlado and Vera returned, they could not find him anywhere. Suppertime arrived, but no Branko. Vera suddenly had a terrible premonition. She began to weep. And Vlado went out into the yard and discovered the small body. Branko had left a childish note saying that this, he felt, was the only honorable course for him because he had disgraced his family.

How strange, down at the bottom of the world with all

its calm and clean repose, its tranquil Fabian Socialism as dated as the plays of Bernard Shaw and as removed from the violence of Marx in Eastern Europe, to read this dreadful news so simply told.

Imagine the aching sadness: the haunted, frightened little boy caught in an apparatus he could never hope to understand, too proud to share his misery with anyone, touchingly pleased, perhaps, with his nobility; imagine the care with which he wrapped that belt around the limb, the deliberate way he must have climbed up on it, that last short look about the dreary back yard and then the jump and the small body struggling to its end below a creaking bough.

And imagine the vast, depthless chasm of horror that opened in his parents' minds, the feeling of unpardonable guilt, the sickening fear that no loyalty to any friend or cause was worth this, the stretching out upon a couch of the small body, the shyly polite lad in his patched hand-me-down clothes, with eyes now staring blankly.

There was the Revolution's child, the little boy who once would haughtily shout: "Where is the car?"

Two weeks after Steve's note I received a tragic letter from Vera (and you must imagine how this was written in that lonely gloom, that penurious apartment, smelling of cabbage, no longer quite so overcrowded, that self-questioning atmosphere of despair.)

The poor thing reproached herself that she could not save Branko, a child full of life, who could not bear misery and lack of essentials. He had perforce dressed worse than other children, getting hand-me-downs from Boro because he was smaller. Vera craved to believe that a second life exists in which she could meet the poor boy again.

And Vlado was ill: war wounds plus an attack of Jackson's epilepsy. He had lost his will to live and work.

They were guarding Boro and Marko day and night. The other children saw Branko as a hero who had the moral strength to leave this unhappy life.

Vera begged me to see that Olga, Vlado's heroic first wife, was honored. Vlado, in 1952, donated 165,000,000 dinars in order to build a hospital under her name. But they had not yet been informed what happened to that money and whether the hospital was built and, if so, whether it bore her name. Vera's letter empowered me to act legally to press for this.

She also begged me to place a marker on Olga's grave, because "administrative difficulties" had prevented them from doing this.

Four weeks later, Vera wrote again. In frantic fear, she said that two years ago an *agent provocateur* had published an account of a fake conversation with Vlado attributing bad things to him. Vlado denied this and could prove that he was not even in Belgrade. But the man was back again. They didn't know what he was preparing, but they did know who he worked for, and knew what that meant—the police. They dared not open the door to anyone.

How sad it was for Vera to be home. She couldn't look through the window into the yard where Branko died just below the room where they ate their meager lunch.

And Marko cried all day for Branko who had made him a boat of wood. They didn't know what to do with it.

A PERORATION

I

Nowadays, at least as I am writing this, it is not unusual to see on the university campuses of Manchester or Oxford or, occasionally, in London at the library of the Royal Institute of International Affairs, a huge, bulky man, generally with several books clutched in his square but astonishingly small hands, hunching along with a somber, determined look. This is Professor Vladimir Dedijer, for whom the gates of freedom were strangely opened by an implacable regime once his little boy had killed himself. And many months after the entire Dedijer family received their passports, Vlado's friend Djilas was quietly released from prison.

One can never prove any connection between Branko's tragedy and the Tito Government's sudden generosity. But the sequence of events is telling; one can only infer that the dictator, who is, after all, a very human man with particular affection for his own young son (by a second marriage), was induced by this blood sacrifice to relax the persecution of his opponents.

The Marshal had always been rather proud that Yugoslavia, unlike other Communist states, did not execute adversaries but punished them in ways far milder than Stalinist Russia or the satellites. He has told me more than once: "At least we are not brutal. No matter how provoked we may feel we do not trump up fake trials or murder those who turn against us."

This undoubtedly is true; and when the regime decided to relent it was not—as in Hungary or Czechoslovakia—a question of rehabilitating the honor of a corpse: live, if unhappy men, were the tangible beneficiaries.

Less than three months after Branko's suicide, his father was allowed to accept the chair offered by Manchester University and later accompanied by an Oxford grant. He was permitted to leave Belgrade with his wife, mother and three smaller children, while Milica, the eldest, was granted a passport to the United States, where she married a young Yugoslav painter. Vlado's brother Steve was allowed to go to Denmark, where he studied as the guest of Niels Bohr, the nuclear scientist. Finally, Djilas left prison and returned to his books, his typewriter, his wife and son and a quiet Belgrade literary life.

The sudden experience of freedom came as a shock to all these people, or so long confined in the Revolution's various compression chambers. Vlado and his family traveled first to Oslo in December, 1959.

The children were very impressed by Norway. Boro told a friend: "In this country the Prime Minister has a salary only twice and a half as much as a qualified worker and only the Foreign Minister has a state-owned car. Many ministers ride bicycles."

When the family passed by a prison, little Bojana exclaimed: "What, prisons in this country. I am so disappointed." The youngest one, Marko, a typical melancholic boy from Bosnia, brooded: "It is so fine for us here, and I am so afraid that someone else may pass away in our family."

Vera, who bore such huge burdens, dreamed almost every night that still another child had died and she had to make preparations for a funeral.

Just after New Year's Day, 1960, I received a letter, this time from the Dedijers' in Manchester where they had spent the holidays with Nye Bevan and his wife, Jenny Lee. Bevan knew he was dying of cancer but was very gallant about it.

That Christmas was very sad. At Asheridge Farm, the English Socialist's home, Jennie and Nye did their best so that the children might enjoy a peaceful Christmas. Although Nye was in great pain, he was with the children for many hours every day. He asked Vlado not to tell the children that he was going to be operated on.

Life went on for the unhappy Dedijers.

Milica married on March 19, 1960, in New York. Mrs. Franklin Roosevelt gave a dinner at her home for Milica and Vaso [the youthful artist bridegroom]. It was very moving. At the end of dinner, a birthday cake was brought in. The day before had been Milica's twentieth birthday.

In October, 1960, Milica ran into trouble with the U.S. immigration authorities but Mrs. Roosevelt, her son, Representative James Roosevelt, Under Secretary of State Chester Bowles and others helped her.

She wrote that she was pleased with the American way of life: "The main thing is that here there is liberty."

My view of Dedijer's political testament: Poor Yugoslavia, it has suffered so much. Now, after the Revolution that engulfed so many, it is resuming its traditional role—just another little Balkan police state that nobody really cares about.

The Revolution has lost its glitter. It promised too

much. It gave the peasants the impression that every little village would have its university and the cows would have gold teeth. Now there is no more enthusiasm. And Tito, poor Tito, he leads the life of old John D. Rockefeller, friendless, lonely, surrounded by toadies.

He was made a fool of by Khrushchev who built his own position in Russia by apologizing for Stalin's 'political' mistakes but never made an ideological peace with Tito. Tito is left with no ideology. First Gomulka [Poland's former Communist chief], now him, being nibbled to death by Moscow.

That is the way Titoism itself deals with its own heretics, like Djilas and others. Maybe one might contend that Stalin was less cruel. He just shot them. This system slowly deprives them of life. It is like Orwell's 1984, but worse.

An old Partisan once said years ago that the Yugoslav Communists had only a certain amount of moral capital, earned during the war, and were using it up too fast.

As for the children, they are slowly learning other things. When told the story of Joan of Arc, a little girl was so horrified to hear that the English had burned her that she wanted to leave England. When told that this all happened five centuries ago, she told her father he was lying. "You just want to comfort me. I know it really happened only yesterday."

Out of politics now, Dedijer must have felt that he was really becoming a historian—which he often thought must be his destiny. Yet he was increasingly puzzled when he saw the world through history's eyes, and not through those of an ideologist.

Everybody in Europe, including Communist Europe,

looks on America as a land with a wonderfully high stand-ard of living, great comfort, lovely, clean girls. Now Khrush-chev proclaims publicly that he will overtake America in this realm of living standards. That is an unwise decision on his part. For this is the one domain in which he can never overtake America. Therefore he will be defeated."

So Dedijer's testament as I see it.

II

And Djilas, the proto-heretic inside Tito's own heresy, the man who attacked Communism's "New Class" and re-signed from it and all its privileges: what has become of this wild knife-wielding mountain poet?

On January 21, 1961, Djilas was finally released from prison and allowed to return to his modest Belgrade apart-ment. Although still prevented from traveling abroad or getting a job in the state-controlled economy, he is rela-tively free, as free as Dedijer was in previous years.

"I cannot be either entirely satisfied or dissatisfied," he says, "as is usual in politics and in reality."

His health, on the whole, despite serious ulcers, survived the rigors of jail. Now he spends most of his time lounging about with Stefka, his second wife, and their son Aleksica. He is determined to keep writing and the government re-turned to him the manuscripts he prepared in prison, after first inspecting them.

Djilas wrote Dedijer expressing his sympathy for Branko's death. He understood how the terrible strain of isolation had "contributed to it."

He added: "I loved him best of all your children; he was outstanding among them. And, finally, I felt his death—

even though indirectly—as the tragedy of our situation."

For Djilas the return to even restricted freedom produced a great internal peace. Once he said: "At this moment the east wind, the Kosava, is blowing; but I'm not cold; I am no longer in prison."

And he also found that "Time, of which I had too much while in prison, has suddenly become too short. Loved ones —whom I was then happy to see once a month—are all at once unbearably absent if they go away for only a minute and no further than the next room."

And where, along the devious, zigzag road of revolution, had Djilas' personal philosophy led him? He wrote to Dedijer: "As far as my views are concerned, that's another question and an extremely complex one. I can say that on some questions my thinking has evolved along your lines, and on others it has changed in some respects, but at bottom there are no fundamental changes.

"In the past few years I have thought a great deal about the past, and about the two of us, and everything seemed unimportant to me beside our friendship—that which is human and essential in it. I felt everything that happened to you, both good and ill, with the utmost of sensitivity and interest. I was very sorry that you had to leave the country, although I regarded that as the wisest and even most human solution under the circumstances. But then, I don't need to remind you of your misfortunes.

"Even the greatest spirits belong to their own era. In fact, the more in accord with their times they are, the greater they are. They introduce moments of passion, interest, and the lessons of the past into their views and their actions.

"During the past few years, although I didn't add to my knowledge—except for modern literature—I believe that I have perfected certain views, or more exactly, certain pages and points of my own understanding of human destiny and history.

"I mean that I have returned and am returning to the unchanging laws of human existence, always different in form and, in the final analysis, intangible, and I regard all social theories as temporary and relative—as the premeditated framework within which certain groups are obliged to struggle under certain already determined conditions.

"Therefore, the task of science (history) appears to me to be only to determine, describe, and define those forms in all their conditions and variety, while everything else is only prophecy, or the paying of debts to one's epoch.

"All this could be described in much more detail and documented if there were time enough, and a good solid advance preparation. My idea can be reduced to Goethe's: all theory is gray, the tree of life alone is evergreen. One must first know one's materials and then build the theories, that is, draw conclusions."

III

We have seen how Vergniaud's prescience applied to Vladimir Dedijer: that immense, resolute, earnest Serb, battered again and again by war, who buried one wife amid clattering battle and saw the second eviscerated by despair. He turned, in loyalty to a friend, against the implacable machine he had himself helped create and which subsequently sought to drain from his wearying soul the final elements of human choice and freedom.

He was in a very real sense saved by another's sacrifice in blood: the pitiful self-immolation of young Branko, which touched the heart of even a heartless mechanism. Dedijer was saved to persevere along the lonely path of individuality, still seeking the goals he now knows are no longer there, unwilling to turn from dreamt-out dreams; but at peace, at last at peace, within himself.

Here is the Resistentialist of that insatiable revolt which gobbles its sponsors as blindly as those it sets out to destroy as enemies; the Resistentialist whose destiny was to think splendid thoughts and fight for them with ruthlessness, but who, as he approached the pit before him, could draw back and resist when he saw his own revolution resuming its traditional sordid role.

Ah, how hard a way to find that the tree of life is evergreen. At least he proved that a brave man can overcome ill fortune and his own misguided errors, that if he adheres to human verity he can for one brief moment turn destiny and oppose fate.

CHAPTER 4

THREE AGAINST FATE

In the period of which I write, when we faced terrible disasters and outlived them, when we did to one another insane and ghastly things, there were fine people on earth. There were splendid men and splendid women aboard in my time and not all of them were famous. But how they suffered, loved, endured.

Around us grind vast movements which we cannot comprehend, movements which turn us into beasts. Science propels us to the stars above while we, on our glum planet, spin eroding into the sun, eroding as life strips us naked and, too often, ugly.

And yet how we struggle to survive, how we cling to our ideals and see them tormented one by one, how we worship at the feet of false gods until they immolate us on their altars. This is the age of the Resistentialist, who, uncomprehending, will not yield.

What is the earmark of the Resistentialist? Courage. And what is courage? It is an absence of cowardice, a willingness, at last, to face the facts; an acceptance of fate, a readiness to meet disaster proudly and on equal terms. When the toast drops butter side down you pick it up and eat it.

My God, how awkward one can be when one wants to

tell a tale and prove a point. In these three true novellas I have chosen my text—and now the sermon: preach, now, brother, preach.

Ours is the age that mocks the Hegel-Nietzsche legend, Hegel's "world-historical men, the Heroes of an epoch," Nietzsche's "strong men, the masters" who "regain the pure conscience of a beast of prey; monsters filled with joy." Once more rendered humble, perhaps by the dreadful formulas we fabricate, we learn again the lessons of Socrates and Milarepa that self-conquest is worth more than world-conquest; that, in the end, no crutch is needed for the man of independence, pride and tolerance. This is the sermon of my three novellas.

I suppose what I am trying to prove is that a man, a real man, should be able to stand up in the worst of storms, even if he doesn't believe in anything, in anything at all, even if he has been stripped of all his credos but tolerance and pride; even alone, quite utterly alone, and in a desert where no one and nothing will register his pain or note his bravery; we who are condemned to solitude.

What is it, what inherent force, that makes such a man go on? The heroes of these tales deliberately searched for trouble; and still they persevered, all three. They played a gallant game against the dealer with a stacked deck.

Ripper and Dedijer stood in the whirlwind like gnarled oaks; Dupont bent like a reed; but none of the trio was uprooted. Ripper, when dead, was betrayed by his religion and mocked by his philosophy. Dedijer was betrayed by the spurious dream he cherished and Dupont let down by the woman for whom he sacrificed his honor.

Not any of these men was great in the usual mundane sense; let us acknowledge this. The mark they made is small: Dupont, the gallant little weakling, who spun and perhaps today still spins like a leaf in a rain-swept gutter; Ripper, inherently a side-tracked artist, too *engagé* in life itself, at best a painter of the second rank; and Dedijer, the stout, stubborn mastiff, historian of a noble nation which history itself will regard as insignificant.

We may read many lessons in these stories. The lesson of Ripper is that you must never compromise, even at the end; you do not deal with what you fought so long as it survives. Diels, the man who tortured and humiliated him, was dead; but not his friends, nor the malignant system which they served and in the vestiges of which the foolish Ripper settled; poor Rip, the victim in death of what he had fought so savagely in life.

The lesson of Dedijer is that a man may never, if even for a moment, abandon tolerance; that no faith which is a blind faith is worth honoring; and that he who escapes whole from fanaticism is both a noble man and fortunate, no matter the price he pays for freedom.

The lesson of Dupont is simply that there are some burdens too great for any man to bear—and yet they are borne. There are some crimes for which no punishment is just, for they are committed on the basis of foredoomed guilt; the chance of innocence, the innocence of choice, does not exist. When human laws become as immutable as the law of gravity, they cannot, in a sense, be violated.

And the lesson of Dupont is perhaps that if one perseveres the wheel may turn a bit. As he said in his farewell letter: "I have been in a lot of troubles, working like a slave all the time. I wouldn't care for me, that's the men's share in life. . . . I can't say I am unlucky, for I fell on the most understanding and courageous woman there's on earth." This, the bittersweet reward for the man betrayed by fate and love with scars healed above unhealing wounds: a brave man aided by a gentle woman can recover even from deception, shame and ignominy.

Consider the Ripper, a man who might so easily, like other Austrians of his class, have become a Fascist, treading the path first limned so giddily by Prince Starhemberg; and yet, once drawn into the struggle, who fought on the side of freedom with such intrepidity. How does a man have his flesh torn by bombs and bullets twenty-seven times, his skull smashed, his back beaten, and yet survive integral and intact?

"Die and suffer we do," as he confided to that superb and intimate war journal, "willingly or unwillingly, because that is all there is to it. . . .

"And when we go back we shall be more frightened than we were the first time But we all go back because there is nothing else to do."

This is the humanist. For he acknowledged: "There is a sadness in being a man, but it's a proud thing too. . . . We are very conscious of having only one life to live and how precious it is."

Nor, now that he is dead, should we forget what he

wrote to his mother in 1934 from the agonies of a concentration camp when even death, to lesser people, might have seemed a blessing:

"I will remain strong no matter what. I am still beginning my life and will realize some day that I have not lived in vain. . . . The best of life lies in good memories. And I am happy. Be happy also."

We are happy.

And Dedijer, when the blinkers of fanaticism had been whisked from his eyes, confessed without embarrassment: "I see that everything is not black and white. There are many grays in the picture." Mild, one may say, and unprofound, neither original nor penetrating; but oh, so important when learned the hard way.

Unlike the turncoats who are a praised and humiliating feature of our era, Dedijer needed no new crutch to replace the one he had discarded. "I am just out of one 'Catholic church,'" he told me, "and I don't want to get into another. I suppose, ideologically speaking, I want to be a free-lance."

Therefore, he recognized: "I see the need for tolerance and now I am learning tolerance for everyone. . . . This has been an excellent moral experience for me."

Within this new tolerance, he retained his pride: "Don't feel sorry for me. I have learned much. And remember this, Cy: Whatever occurs, I am not going to eat dirt. If you have to eat dirt once in your life you will have to say it is good forever."

And Dupont, that anonymous and insignificant pawn,

unable to express his inner sorrows even to himself, the brave man faced with the impossible question to which there was no answer; nor could there ever be. Fortune alone impelled him toward Hemingway, who could thereafter testify: "He was as brave a man as I ever knew."

Hemingway said: "Michel Dupont carried out greatly useful reconnaissance missions with much courage and bravery. The officers of the American 4th Infantry Division often praised him for his bravery, his zeal and his intelligence . . . during one of the most difficult periods of the war."

To which General Lanham added: "To my mind, this obscure Frenchman—the true little man of Europe—epitomizes the fearful travail of the age in which we live. Certainly now more than ever all men would do well to remember the essential truth of the old French proverb: 'To understand all is to forgive all.'"

So there, in this dismal age, on the brink of a flaming future, these men, tarnished by cruelty, deceived by illusions, remained intact, which is in itself a triumph. Stubbornly they fought against huge odds with no ally, in the end, but their own resolution in their own weak selves.

They were incurious about death, often as they faced it, as one is incurious about the night. Yet how magnificent was the noontime of the day in which they dwelled.

Take heart, my friends, take courage from these Resistentialists and share their compassion for each other and yourselves.

POSTSCRIPT

During the period between the writing and final publication of UNCONQUERED SOULS much has happened to the characters involved. Poor Hemingway, such a splendid man and writer, took his life when he realized he could never hope to cure the mental illness that was destroying his vast talent, if it had not already totally destroyed it. Buck Lanham has retired but, after his great spirit was wounded by the suffering of his wife who finally died, he has found late happiness by a second marriage to a charming woman. And hapless Michel, the unwilling and wholly anonymous hero of "The Bravest Collaborator"— he has disappeared. I have no idea whether he is still alive although he would today be in his relatively early sixties. But he was a bad luck figure, cursed with the need to make impossible choices and to survive when he did not wish to survive. If he exists, in some obscure and almost certainly miserable haven, I fear he is haunted by more ghosts than any man should have to face.

All of the Yugoslavs mentioned save Olga Dedijer, who had already died years earlier on a battlefield, have experienced great change: with the single exception of Marshal Tito himself who, an old, old man, was still in 1972 at his country's helm. Ranković, the police boss, is in disgrace and out of power. Steve Dedijer lives in Sweden, a member of the Lund University faculty. He has married a Swedish girl and made a new life and family for himself. Milica is a vigorous young married woman in California. Djilas has earned literary and philosophical fame abroad but is rarely permitted to travel outside Yugoslavia. He is embittered with the political system for which he fought so desperately and the regime does whatever it can to isolate him from his countrymen. Not even his short stories or his Serbo-Croatian translation of Milton's *Paradise Lost*, painstakingly worked upon in prison, can appear in Yugoslavia. But at least he is no longer in jail. He, his wife and his son lead a comfortable life in Belgrade, surrounded by books and paintings, and I still cherish the hope that one of these days he will be permitted to accept my standing invitation to come and shoot birds on the little Greek island where we have a house.

By far the most tragic of the heretical figures encountered in these pages is Vlado Dedijer. In the end, he and Vera returned with their surviving children to Yugoslavia where he is now professor at a provincial university and has made a name for himself as a historian. From time to time he is allowed to travel abroad (unlike the proto-heretic, Djilas) and he has visited several European countries and the United States. But he suffered an unbelievable misfortune when another one of his sons died a violent death, victim of a mountaineering mishap in the peaks of Slovenia. Too much unhappiness has been instilled within his huge frame and the dark night of lovely Vera's soul.

From the twisted fabric of these terrible episodes, all of

which occurred during and after World War II, it is possible to discern certain patterns. Each of the main characters involved was a demonstrably courageous human being, brave enough among other things to change his mind and suffer on a matter of principle. The Dedijers and Djilas could so easily have retained the privileges and power of that New Class the description of which, in a Communist society, first made Milovan world-famous (and also first got him into serious trouble as what, in other societies, might have been called a "traitor" to his class). But they preferred to stick to their ideals and, in the process, to become more understanding human beings. For suffering is an inspired teacher of humanity.

Ripper might well have remained loyal to the meaningless Austrian aristocracy into which he was born or, for that matter, might all too easily have found an outlet for his adventurous tastes in the Nazi militarism that engulfed the entire Teutonic world during its heyday after the *Anschluss*. Instead, he found truth early, through his perceptive soul and huge heart, and he devoted his life to fighting terror and dictatorship when he wasn't depicting it or the bruises it caused with his pastels, oils and etchings.

The unknown is Michel. Almost certainly he never had a special talent or an original idea worth recording. His individuality was spawned by the agony of war and he became a fearless fighting man only by resentment. And then he was too unfortunate to escape the grim wave of vengefulness that swept France right after the conflict, a wave no doubt intensified by the fact that so many Frenchmen knew they had collaborated with the enemy in their hearts, if not by their actions, and therefore felt summoned to erase their own guilt by attaching it to others. Thousands of shrewd, wise or influential persons among them were able to lie low for long enough to avoid this brutal reaction. None of those adjectives applied to Michel Dupont. Instead of earning a decoration (Lanham wrote in a sworn statement: "If Monsieur Dupont had been an American soldier instead of a French volunteer combating as an irregular, I would have cited him personally for his bravery in combat") Michel was sent to prison.

Another trait these Resistential heroes shared in common was that of loneliness, exile from their fellow-men, either self-sought or enforced. Here we may even include Hemingway who lived so much of his life in Europe or in Cuba, though he came home to die. Vlado Dedijer seemed to contemplate voluntary exile for a considerable period but has adjusted his solitary soul to uneasy Yugoslavia. Steve, on the other hand, is now to all intents and purposes a Swede. Ripper had already chosen Spain for his home before he died: an odd choice, in a way, since it was still governed by the Franco regime against whose coming to power he had fought so hard. And Dupont was more or less driven into the worst kind of exile by an unsympathetic society that refused to accept the return to its midst of a man officially branded a collaborator. His kind of exile was the most degrading: anonymous disappearance. And what can be worse, Voltaire inquired, than to be obscurely hanged?

It is odd to note that almost every character in this book

was either himself a creative artist (and certain among them, like Hemingway and Djilas, of notable mark) or closely associated with some aspect of the artistic world. Even Michel Dupont enters this story on the fringes of cinema, as a film editor. Lanham could well have been a writer instead of a soldier; he had the talent and it is a pity he never applied himself to it. All his life he has been a friend of writers. Bruce, of course, in addition to being as fine a diplomat as the United States has produced since Benjamin Franklin, also wrote an excellent history of the American Presidents. Vlado Dedijer is the author of many books and Steve has written much on scientific matters, ranging from sociology and ecology to nucleonics. Ripper was not only a gifted painter and etcher but also was gaining considerable fame for the jewels he designed just before death struck him down.

Another strange coincidence is that practically everybody mentioned had had at least two wives: Michel Dupont was let down by the first who left him while he was serving that fearfully unjust jail sentence; Vlado was married to two of the loveliest girls in a land renowned for its fair women, the beautiful dark Olga, with the face of an old Greek icon, and the beautiful golden Vera, shattered by a succession of family disasters. Steve Dedijer also had two wives, one who quit him when he was being persecuted for a combination of loyalty to his brother and independence of his own ideological views, and one who lives happily with him and their children in South Sweden. Ripper was first wed to a highly intelligent Jewish girl from Germany who managed to survive the ghastliness of

Ravensbrück concentration camp. When she emerged they divorced in amiable circumstances and Rip acquired the magnificent Avi. Even, one might point out, such background figures as Djilas, Lanham and Hemingway had more than one wife. Milovan divorced his first, the doughty revolutionary known by her maiden name as Mitra Mitrovica, before marrying Stefanie who has cared for him so tenderly during his years of vicissitude. Lanham lost his first wife, Pete, to cancer; Hemingway had four. All these men loved well and all of them, to one or another degree, wisely.

Moreover, although they were not all revolutionists in the full ideological sense, they were all rebels, either born or made into such by circumstance. The Dedijers, Djilas, Tito, Ranković and almost every Yugoslav of the generation embracing them at its extreme limits were revolutionaries, at least those who survived. What betrayed Djilas and the Dedijers was the permanence of their individual revolutions; they had not rebelled against one form of tyranny to willingly accept another, even one they themselves had helped to fabricate. Ripper was a rebel against society as such, against a world to which he belonged by inheritance but not by spirit. If anything he was an anarchist. Had he been born three generations earlier or one generation later he might well have been a nihilist. And poor Dupont, he was in no sense a willing rebel against anything. Indeed, he was even prepared to accept the dead burden of Nazi conquest and stultified occupation by a brutal system. But he was forced despite himself, almost against himself, to revolt against a system determined to destroy those he loved best. In the end it destroyed him as well; destiny's whirlwind was too great for him.

One could go on making comparisons, finding common traits among the Resistentialists, and draw the conclusion that these men, of approximately the same age bracket, born in Europe in time to be tossed about by its most tumultuous upheaval, had in common the sheer determination to survive, an innate courage that perhaps they themselves did not know existed in them. Yet how contrasting were the forms this innate courage chose in order to express itself: enthusiastically with Ripper, violently with Djilas, grimly with Dedijer and resentfully with Dupont.

Surely none of them may be considered lucky. The talent potential of Ripper and Dedijer was seriously weakened or cut off short by events. That Djilas was able to produce creative triumphs was thanks only to his vigorous resolution which made the most of the imposed inactivity of sordid prison confinement. Dupont, alas, had nothing original to give the world; what he did manage to contribute from his poor stock of vitality was squeezed out of him by the juggernaut that crushed his country. Indeed, of all these eponymous heroes of Resistentialism, perhaps Ripper alone could with justice be called a happy man and, prematurely though it came, he was even happy in his death, with his wife, among friends, on his Mediterranean island, even though the dreadful, ridiculous events that accompanied his interment could only disgust and sadden those who loved him and would have inspired howls of ribald laughter in Rip himself.